FIRST LAW
OF HOLES

"*First Law of Holes* feels like an entire universe of characters and experiences. Infinite, expanding and dotted with stars."

—Charmaine Wilkerson, author of *Black Cake*

FIRST LAW
OF HOLES

— NEW AND SELECTED STORIES —

MEG POKRASS

DZANC
BOOKS

DZANC BOOKS

2580 Craig Rd.
Ann Arbor, MI 48103
www.dzancbooks.org

Library of Congress Cataloging-in-Publication Data Available Upon Request

ISBN: 9781950539987
First US edition: September 2024
Interior design by Michelle Dotter
Cover art by Lou Beach
Cover design by Steven Seighman

Grateful acknowledgement to the following literary magazines:
*Electric Literature, Northwest Review, Atticus Review, Cleaver, JMWW, Six Sentences,
Gone Lawn, Passages North, FiveSouth, New World Writing*

Grateful acknowledgement to the following presses:
Anthologies: Flash Fiction America (W. W. Norton, 2015), New Micro: Very Short
Fiction (W. W. Norton, 2018), Flash Fiction American (W. W. Norton, 2023), The
Best Small Fictions 2018 (Braddock Avenue Books), The Best Small Fictions 2023
(Sonder Press), Alcatraz (Gazebo Books)
Collections:
Damn Sure Right (Press 53, 2011), *Bird Envy* (Harvard Bookstore, 2014), *Cellulose
Pajamas* (Blue Light Press, 2015), *The Dog Looks Happy Upside Down* (Etruscan
Press 2016), *Alligators at Night* (Ad Hoc Fiction 2018), *The Dog Seated Next to Me*
(Pelekinesis, 2019)

Printed in the United States of America

10 9 8 7 6 5 4 3 2 1

CONTENTS

For Miles, Hannah, and Sian

Maude: "You know, at one time, I used to break into pet shops to liberate the canaries. But I decided that was an idea way before its time. Zoos are full, prisons are overflowing . . . Oh my, how the world still dearly loves a cage."

—Maude, From *Harold and Maude*, 1971

THE PRODUCER

The ninety-year-old Producer had a hole in his heart. A shaky, un-patchable hole. He wanted me to fill it with kisses, candy, and jokes. I handed him a travel-size Mars bar that I got on the plane.

"Only a monkey," he said, "would offer this old sack of bones a gift from the Red Planet."

He said this because of my newly red hair. He liked to run his skinny fingers through it. I called him "The Producer" because he had always wanted to produce a movie. Sometimes he asked me to write one. Told me to create a character role just for him, and to make him younger, less shaky, less married, without Parkinson's. That was easy, as I imagined him a younger person.

The nickname "Monkey" rubbed off on me. There was a gullible monkey on my shoulder, enjoying the stories he told me about his terrible home life. How his wife carried a loaded pistol around the house, even in her pjs.

"She never puts it away anymore." He winked. What a horrible person she was, I told myself, kissing his shivery lips.

* * *

"That blouse is very flattering on you," The Producer said, his face half fallen. It was the same blouse I had worn every other night in the dining room. I wondered if he had had a mini-stroke in his sleep. Half of his face looked younger than the other half, less percep-tive. He gazed at me as if I alone provided gravity.

The hotels we stayed in had very good food. We would eat in the dining rooms, and middle-aged businessmen would stare with disgusted expressions as the two of us nibbled appetizers and sipped rhubarb gin. They thought he had to be a great-uncle or a grandfather, so why was I wearing such a low-cut, decadent blouse? Why were his eyes gripping the rise of my cleavage as if he was pulling himself out of some brackish lake?

He's The Producer, and I'm in love with him, I wanted to say. Give me a break, I didn't have a dad! I wanted to scream. They would offer me a weak nod, as if to say, if he croaks tonight, I'm around.

* * *

My story is filled with love tragedies. I told The Producer all about them. "You should write a screenplay about it," he said, and this cheered me up.

My strong, young boyfriends would eventually say that they saw our relationship as a weakness. I never knew what they meant. Their muscular legs would take off for runs or bike rides in the early morning. They were running away from me, my mother once said, because often, they didn't return.

For example, my young husband disappeared after going for a long, mindful ultra-run. "I like the look of that path," he said, and I never saw him again. I knew there were mountain lions around, but they never found his bones. Thankfully I heard from him a few years later. He wrote me a postcard from Jakarta to say that his knees, hips, and spine had finally given out.

"That's what unhappiness does to you," he wrote.

By the time I turned twenty-seven, I was tired of the young ones, their perfect bodies and deeply unsatisfied souls.

* * *

When I first met The Producer, I had just arrived at a hotel with my dog. I was still married, but my husband had been missing for years. When he hugged me in the lobby of the hotel, I tried not to cry.

"You are tattered and shabby," he said, or maybe I imagined it. His skin was yellowed and fragile to the touch.

"I like your face," I said.

"I like your dog," he said.

We took the elevator up to his hotel room. He put on a Lucinda Williams song. He had an iPad he didn't know how to use. He said the one thing he was confident about was the music app. "Somehow, I can make it sing," he said.

The song that plays in my head these days, when I remember The Producer, is "Something About What Happens When We Talk." I felt it was corny the first time he played it for me. But now that he's gone, I miss the talks we had, how much he liked my dog, and how it always felt like he was calling to me from someplace close, but also very far away.

* * *

The last time I saw him, he perched on the sofa of our hotel room as if he was ready to fly.

"We are not the same age," he said. This seemed like an obvious fact, and one that might have been noted already.

"I am not worried about it," I said. "Are you?"

I took his hand, and it was cold. I wanted to say, please don't fret about nonsense. I yanked him off the sofa, right into my arms. We danced to Lucinda Williams. I felt sad that he had said it and was shivering a bit. He held me tight as a twenty-year-old but felt as light as a paper doll.

"How did your wife find out?" I asked. The phone started to ring. I knew it was the last time we would ever meet.

"Don't let her shoot you," I said. He was so weightless, I could have carried him home in my arms.

FAMILY SECRETS

There was a story about a woman who kept her husband and her daughters on a leash. It wasn't the kind of story you tell at a party. It was a kind of unspoken understanding between growing-up sisters.

There are neighbors we will never know, my father says. Old stories about them bloom like unexplained flowers in a parched-out garden.

Here in our city, nobody knows each other.

My sisters say there are stories about us too. We laugh. We think we are mostly okay now. We talk about our silly lives together as if we are able to stand above them and watch ourselves from the edge. The labor we do here feels necessary. We relocate our father from the living room to another room when he can no longer stand up.

Your mother used to keep us on a leash, our father says, clearing his throat. Then he sits down and thinks again. We bring him a cup of hot water. *Tell us a bit more,* we say. He likes his tea without a bag, just a tiny squirt of lemon. *I have never needed much of a leash, myself,* he says.

There is a joke about a horror story about a mother who never stopped walking. She walked her leashed daughters to the edge of a cliff and told them to jump. Then she pulled and saved the one who didn't understand what was really expected of her.

We work and we grow up and we learn how we are safest when standing away from the edges of things. We point at the house where the mother and her leashed daughters lived. It is the one that resembles a submarine.

Houses like ours, houses on this block, are mostly sunken into

the ground. There are rooms below and rooms above, and the children live in the darker areas. My sisters and I were taken into the
custody of our father.

IF YOU WANT TO BE LOVED, LOVE

1. "If you want to be a horse, be a horse." Her father said this when he talked about the family infrastructure, how weak it was. When she was little, she wanted to become strong as a horse to make him happy, so she tried to become one, but it never worked.

2. Later, there was the shock of loving a man with the soul of a tree. She had always wanted to be a bird, at least in her dreams. But when she was with this man, she didn't want to be anything, she only wanted to fly to him.

3. The doctor told her if she wanted to be loved, next time she needed to *love*. She didn't understand what he meant so she stared into his eyes. They looked like the eyes of a sad, old horse, a horse that knew in its heart it was probably going to become glue for some rich child's special art project. This was the day she fell in love with her doctor.

4. "If you want to be a horse, be a horse," she said to her son when he tried on his Halloween costume and stared in the mirror as if he had failed at being scary. "How can I be a horse?" the child asked. "Stand there like this," she said, "as if you are stuck in the middle of a field, but it doesn't worry you."

5. When her father walked into the ocean and never came out, her mother started painting birds. It felt like a dream, her mother waving a paintbrush at six a.m. Blackbirds and sparrows all over the kitchen walls and her mother up early enough to catch a worm. "Your father was upset about our infrastructure," she said. "You know he would have hated me doing this."

6. When she became an artist, she gave up the idea of being okay. She stood in her kitchen and remembered her mother surrounded by birds. Her son, who had been a successful horse on Halloween, watched her with love in his unknowable eyes.

MATCHPOINT

She flew back into her husband's childhood as a bird. Heard the hollow throp of a tennis ball and watched him play against his pink-shirted father. His father gripped a martini in one hand, racquet in the other. Sunburnt, black-coffee grin, her husband's father younger than her husband was now.

"Don't tell Mom, okay, Einstein?" he said.

She watched the father-in-law lose at tennis, as if racing against the sun. Saw the husband beaming, taking an internal bow. Saw him follow his father back inside, watching from a corner of the living room while his father cried.

"I'm stuck here in this body, Einstein," his father said. "Don't be snide."

Saw him pour himself another drink, saw him kick the dog— saw all of what her husband saw. Wondered. Was this why?

Watched him in his childhood bedroom. A twelve-year-old assassin, sprinkling talcum powder on his feet. They were already wide, with plush, feminine toes. Watched him stick the edge of a cuticle scissors into the flesh around his ankle bone, follow his own trail of blood to the windowsill.

There she stood, a dumb sad bird, already sure he would open the window and let her in.

CHAMPION PIGEON

That time I took a train to Cornwall and sat on the beach thinking about nobody. That time I thought about finding a dog. That time I remembered nothing about the house in the city, the home my ex and I used to feel happy in. That time I decided life was about this moment and the next, one solo beach adventure at a time. That time I stood up and kicked off my flip-flops. That time I stood up and waved to invisible dolphins. That time and one other time after that, I missed nobody and nothing.

* * *

The days were all about sandwiches. Which ones to enjoy and which ones to improve on. One sandwich had floppy bread and stringy cheese. Another sandwich had too many seeds and not enough meat. My sandwich-making skills were depleted. My life as an adventurer living alone in her kitchen felt unhappy. Some days, even the normal things felt they needed forgiveness. Some days, I wanted to take a train ride to Cornwall and stop trying to make sandwiches. To eat at cafés with a traveler's smile.

* * *

The man from Alaska texted to say he was experiencing boredom. I told him I was experiencing a similar thing. Is boredom an actual thing? he said. Yes, boredom is certainly a thing, I said. He asked me what I was cooking up for dinner. Shrimp ragout with yellow lentils and shiitake mushrooms, I lied. That sounds fantastic, he said. Damn right, and I'm somebody lucky, I said. After that, I went into the kitchen to prepare myself a non-gooey sandwich. This time, I added fresh basil leaves for kicks, sprinkled pepper on healthy bread, hoping it would calm everything down.

* * *

There was that time I heard an actual scream. It was no longer living in my head. I ran outside to see where it came from. I looked around the quiet cul-de-sac, saw nothing. The man across the way was outside, feeding his pigeons. The pigeons were champions of living in cages. I wondered about striking up a conversation. How are the birds today? I might say. But then I remembered the echo of a scream. How easy it could be to wear a disguise, I thought. I stared at the man. Why did the people around here have such vapid smiles, yet nobody said a word? I decided a simple encounter could easily become one big accident and went back into my house.

* * *

In his text, the man from Alaska said a visit would be like a winter gift. "It's warmer there than here, at least," he said. I could hear a pigeon cooing outside the window while his positive thoughts chirped on, and my heartbeat grew regular. But later, I turned off my phone. Life became simple, walking outside and back in the house, looking for mail that had yet to arrive. I probably needed an office, I thought. I needed to get out of the house, a house can become an enemy. That time I realized the man's visit would not cheer me up. That time I felt only a tiny bit of shame for not encouraging him. How much I wanted to visit a relative, one who no longer lived on this earth.

* * *

On the beach in Cornwall, I decided living alone was all about imagination. I thought about bringing home a puppy. All of the beautiful reasons to do it. I imagined the kind of friendship I might have with a gifted dog. But then I remembered how the best dogs weren't terribly smart. You don't want a smart one, a friend said. What you want is the kind who won't take over your life. I would research dumb dogs as soon as I got home, I told myself. I put back on my flip-flops. They hurt my toe skin, but I was becoming tough. I would not think of the old house, the divorce. I would grow old in my cage like a champion pigeon.

THE HAPPIEST COUPLE IN THE WORLD

1. She grew old with her partner, an accountant who she first became attracted to because he was safe. "I love you deeply, I want to live the rest of my life with you," he said on each anniversary, when he appeared in the living room in a flamenco pose, a rose between his teeth.

2. He had always understood how much she hated parties, why she distrusted people who were too nice, why she wanted to adopt a pet just as soon as one of the other ones died. "Maybe we can adopt a reptile next time," he would say. "Or a rabbit."

3. They lived in a cheap and practical town and had very few cultural needs. She settled in well, made good solid friends who came over and shared winter recipes.

4. She learned how to knit, to quilt, to sew. She had two grown children, both easygoing professionals with comfortable smiles.

5. When he slept, he snored like a soft old bear. In the middle of the night, he offered her the warm, dark cave of his shoulder. Understood how much she needed to feel like a secret to him, even though they'd been married for years.

FIRST LAW OF HOLES

"Before he became a clown, he was a bit light-footed," Mom said. "Your father could slip away in the middle of a funeral and nobody would notice."

These were stories I collected about Dad, who I barely remembered from childhood. My father, Mom said, was always doing handstands and forward flips for anybody who had time to stand there and watch him.

"What was he like in regular ways?" I asked. "What did he like to eat, for instance?"

"He loved a good steak," Mom said. "In fact, this was one of the only normal things about him."

In gymnastics class, the teacher took me aside, let me know my flexibility was excellent, and on top of that, I had potential as a mime. In this way, I resembled my father. She'd read about him. His clownmanship, at this point, was legendary. I knew this was serious praise, but what did being a flexible mimic get a person in life? It wasn't something a person needed to be good at.

"When you were just a few molecules in my stomach, your father let me know he was interested in clown school," Mom said. "I hoped he was having a midlife moment."

At the dinner table, her face was crumpled. As usual, the rice was overcooked, mushy and useless. She didn't eat her own cooking, and it was easy to see why. I splashed it with soy sauce and gobbled it up.

Really, Mom was humorless. A thin and ropy woman whose job was cleaning for wealthy people. She worried about my future. I was barely thirteen, and already men were winking at me, clowning around with me, hoping to get me to take them seriously.

Mom said, "Sad, what the human condition does to people like your father, how they find their way into circus tents."

I told myself someday I'd marry an artist, not just a bad husband like Dad.

* * *

I married at seventeen, much to my mother's dismay. At that point, she was so thin it was hard to take her seriously, and I was determined to make it easier for her. I'd found myself a professional circus clown with a fingernail smile.

And I can't deny it. Chuckles made me laugh. Back then, he was like a scoop of tangy sherbet. Healthy. But not ridiculously so. I'd wake up to the sandpaper feeling of his morning stubble between my legs, just one of the pleasures of loving a people-pleaser.

I signed on with the circus troupe as a part-time contortionist. I didn't expect to devote my life to it. I had plenty of time to think it over.

When Mom was still alive, the idea of me living in a circus caravan cavorting with freaks and geeks infuriated her. So I promised I'd never live in a caravan, I'd live a calm and normal life she'd approve of.

"I'm not the gypsy type," I lied, hugging her, her ribs pressing into my heart. She told me my father was living with an East Coast troupe, married to a famous freak known as "Plasticeena."

"Your dad married a freak and a half. Her body is made of recycled milk jugs," she said. "Maybe with me out of the picture, you two might become chummies."

Even Chuckles had heard of Plasticeena. Boy, was he impressed.

"Wowzah," he said. "Intimidating."

"Indeed."

He showed me a photo of the plastic woman plunging a sword

down her translucent throat.

Behind that throat was a tired-looking clown in a wheelchair, and I recognized my father.

Soon after, I found my father's address and wrote to him. Told him Mom was terminally ill.

He wrote back to me and said he was a fulfilled man, part of Plasticeena's medical team. "Since my terrible accident under the Big Top, I teach the clowns to clown," he said. "This is something I can do quite well from a seated position! I teach them how to make horse-lip sounds and how to yawn the stress out of their bodies. I feel like I've found my tribe," Dad wrote. Not a word about Mom. Not even, "I'm sorry."

* * *

Chuckles was broke. "A beautiful pigeon like you really needs nothing more than a rhinestone cap, and you already have one," he said with a sad little smirk.

But he was wrong. I needed more than what I had.

That night I met Olga, a new contortionist. She looked a lot like me, only sexier, with gleaming chestnut hair. Both of us were walking in the same direction, hoping for an invisible net. So, we hooked up near the lion cage, feeling sorry for the big sad cats while sharing the same sky-blue cotton candy. She licked it and then I licked it. We laughed and we licked it again.

We wandered the circumference of the circus together, holding fingers, pretending to be children and ignoring the clowns.

Chuckles was aging quickly, but time was still on my side. He had back issues, neck issues, sadness issues, and charisma issues. So many parts of him were deflating. "Let's go meet your father, I'd love to know him. Let's show him our acts!" he said. Chuckles believed Dad might be able to help by exposing him to a new audience.

But the thing was this: I hadn't seen Dad since I was five and felt frightened of my recycled plastic stepmother.

I tried not to think about any of it. I found myself talking to Mom again, in my dreams.

"Tethering your life to a clown is like eating chocolate pizza," Mom said. "You're going to vomit it out."

She felt so alive to me. I knew she was right.

* * *

"That smart-assed clown is a limp-assed rat," Franz the strong man said. I'd become a guest in my marriage, smiling from a polite corner of the room.

He winked at me, picked me up, carried me around. I enjoyed being the strong man's juggling ball. Olga dug it, too. He juggled the two of us as if we were baby animals.

And it was inevitable. My sense of duty to Chuckles was drawing to a halt. He wandered the caravans at night looking for drinking buddies, bullying the tightrope walker to come out with him.

"We're all guests here in this world of woe," Chuckles brayed, slumped like a toadstool at three in the morning, the breeze blowing his thinning hair around like a tumbleweed.

"His scalp looks shiny enough to skate on," my Olga said over coffee. This made me laugh. I needed to laugh.

I had snuck into her caravan while Chuckles was singing Ethel Merman tunes to the feral cats. We pooled our resources under her gypsy comforter. I dreamed about us living in Manhattan, knotting and unknotting ourselves on an Upper East Side balcony while sharing a salmon bagel.

"Two contortionists are better than one," Franz agreed, as if together Olga and I could become a Hercules knot.

"Well said, Franz. You owe that clown nothing," Olga said, her long arm tightening around my waist.

* * *

And so, on our tenth anniversary under a fingernail moon, I asked Chuckles for a separation. "Why have you stopped loving me?" he cried like a whiny child. Mom would be proud of me, I thought.

I said to Chuckles what she used to say about my father: "The first law of holes is to stop digging."

FAMILY HOLE

After Jeff Friedman

There's a hole in our family, but we can't find it. All three of us go hunting for it with flashlights, searching for places a hole might hide. We come up with nothing, and my wife makes popcorn to cheer us up. Our kid is standing on a skateboard in the living room. "Let's see if I can skate over it with my eyes closed," he says, because he likes to be a hero.

We scour the closets and hard-to-reach places. We investigate boxes of old family photos and Christmas cards, hoping to spot a glimpse of the hole in years past. My wife looks at me intently. "I looked younger then," she sighs. Is the hole new, or has it been here all along? I wonder.

Finally, I decide we're better off not knowing. "Let's put this hole obsession away for now," I say. My wife, who has been reading articles about holes, agrees with me. "Holes have their own logic," she says. As the days drip past, we feel our hole moving a little bit closer. And when our son goes off to college, it grows larger and more invisible than the one we had before.

WATERMARKS

Happily Married

There were times many years ago, long before she got ill, when they did amazing things with their small house, filled it with animals and warmth—sweet spotted dogs and sofa cats, lop-eared rabbits and parakeets, all beautifully messy—and you could see if you looked with narrowed eyes that paint was peeling, water stains forming in corners like wounds, but they were a living kind of proof of devotion, and how humans were as trusting as small, helpless critters you didn't need to be wary of, him next to her on the caving sofa when not driving her to doctor's appointments.

Cracks

He stayed right there next to her on the caving sofa until somehow, one day, he started smoking again, cracked their van on the way to somewhere else, stinking from cologne, wearing tight-fitting jeans as if to shrinkwrap his situation, returning to her with soothing throat lozenges like a dog with a duck in its mouth and with a gleaming crack in their chariot.

Spider-Legged Smiles

After which he couldn't accompany her to doctor's appointments. New watermarks spread out on their ceiling and you could see by his blow-dried hair and his spider-legged smiles that he had befriended a widowed neighbor. Offered to paint her walls.

"I'm more generous than I look, Hon, see if you can fault me for wanting to help," so that when an even younger one came along he could see inside her cleavage, like a child staring into a secret cave.

Prince of a Dog

Inside their damp, water-marked living room, candles finally flickered off, you could spot all of the marks—and now there was only one large dog and five shedding cats and an elderly French lop-eared rabbit on Christmas morning next to the wife on the sofa, and she saw that hers was a shabby rental with a dancing Santa Claus in the corner who appeared deranged, and that the dog next to her on the sofa, with the long paw around her shoulder, was her prince.

HERE WE ARE ON PLANET EARTH

Today at Hendri's Beach, it's all about my best friend and me, tanning on bright red beach towels. One of us has an attractive face. The other has an attractive body. My polliwog body has potential, but there is no way to know how things will turn out.

Blythe's eyes are grey. My eyes are very blue, and they make people *glad to know me*, but I wish mine were unknowable, like Blythe's. Sometimes, there's a language in my friend's eyes that makes me freeze in my tracks, but my goal in this world is to become less uptight. She acts like a million years older than me, even though we share a birthday.

Our bikini tops are off—lying next to us like dead rabbits. We're just a tiny little fleck of what is happening in the world, I tell myself, and our nudity hardly matters. Today there is no question in my mind that Blythe has had sex already.

In other parts of our town, there are more interesting sights: my parents and their awkward divorce, teenagers doing drugs near the bus station, windows being opened to let the fall air in. Ma always loved this season, and she's big on opening the whole house up to welcome it back.

"My shoulder stings," I say, hoping Blythe will offer to rub it with cream.

"Leave things alone," she says.

* * *

Now, a group of boys has found us like artifacts of goodness and are jumping up and down like sand flies, pointing at our bodies, not trying to control their spermy little thoughts.

Saying *Whoa.* Saying *Hi girls.*

"Honk if you believe in Jesus," Blythe replies.

* * *

A middle-aged lady jogs past us on the sand.

"What the hell are you little shits thinking?" Luckily, our sunglasses block her energy out completely. "Do you know what kind of trouble you're asking for? How old are you?"

Blythe laughs, a snarly sound, bats her lashes at me, giggles. She rolls the other way, tits facing the sun. I giggle too, but my gaze gets caught on Blythe's nipples, little pink spaceships hovering over Planet Earth. She arches and flips a fuck-you to the angry woman's face.

Before she jogs away, the woman calls us *dangerous.* Says we deserve what we get.

Says, "Life is not as easy as you think."

CAVITIES

I sat with him in a café and we ate potato salad and drank Italian sodas. All around us, sad-looking people walked happy-looking dogs.

I let him slide his hand over my knee skin. I did not blink, just sat there like an empty driveway. He was in charge. I had one hundred dollars left in my bank account, and my car needed better tires.

"Do you want anything else?" he asked, and I did not.

The potato salad sat heavy in my stomach. Hunger seemed like the tiniest part of being alone. He took me out for two meals each day.

On my birthday, my last pair of reading glasses broke, and I let him have the rest of me. While he did that, I thought about Laffy Taffy, the candy I loved as a kid. How it ruined my teeth, but I wanted it anyway.

IT'S GOOD TO HAVE YOU BACK

On the way back from Folsom State Prison, he slumped in the passenger seat of my car, and it was like the world had handed me a bouquet of overdue roses.

"Thanks for the lift," he said.

"No bother," I said. "It's good to have you back."

For a long time, neither of us said anything. Dad looked swollen, his flesh pale and puffy as bread dough.

"Your freckles have faded," I said.

Dad stared straight ahead, leaning into the sunlight as if trying to make more.

* * *

My boyfriend Al was fat, broken like all the men I'd ever loved. Al's lips were crusted with donut crumbs. He knew I was too weak to love men the right way, and he wanted me to try with my dad more than I did. "Families are what we have," Al said, even though he didn't much care about his own.

So much flesh that had no purpose in this world. Men never made any sense, fading, wilting like roses.

* * *

When I was sixteen, the year he went to prison, my lips were red and my cheeks sweet-smelling. I danced in the living room, dreaming about the kind of bad boys I wanted to love.

"I'm going out," I told my mother, who distrusted most men. She told me Daddy had killed her roses; rode over them with his motorbike before they took him away.

* * *

When I was older, I could see the night sky both ways. We were tiny, and the stars were huge. We were huge, and the stars were pinpricks. My mother probably loved my daddy, but she moved on once he became a regular guy, a guy too fragile to rob another human being of anything. "I'm done with feeling dumb," she said.

She had blood in her cheeks again, and she was messaging a man on the Internet. "Old," she said, "too old to cause any trouble."

I understood, but her words felt false.

I didn't want to see my dad sitting alone all night sunk into his hand-me-down recliner, watching reruns where everything turned out okay at the end of the half hour.

* * *

When Al fucks me, I stare at the ceiling and see myself in the water stains, spreading out unevenly. An old soggy dream. He pushes and moans and says, Tell me how you want it. He's not exactly asking, but I tell him anyway.

I often sniffed the roses my mother grew when my dad was first in prison, until I felt good all the way through, until my insides felt the way the roses smelled.

When Al's done, it's a relief. I can feel the crumbs on my neck. I wipe them away, but it's always too late.

* * *

I'm running toward Daddy in my dreams. I'm saying, Daddy,

you didn't do anything wrong, and I'm holding him, and he's hugging me like I'm a teddy bear who has no voice.

I won't tell you a lie, he says.

I'm growing fast in my dreams, and he's trying to keep me tiny, so he never has to lie to me. Don't grow up, he says, but I'm sitting inside a cardboard box and my limbs are pushing against the sides. I'm making the box leap across the living room. When I step out of it, I have breasts.

Boys follow me into my bedroom like dead-eyed prisoners on their way to the dining hall.

I talk to them about my daddy, his goodness, and the roses my mother planted. I try to make them live, feeding and tending them for the rest of my life.

THE MISSING LINK

Carny running the break-the-plate game won't tell you you're a winner, but you know when you are. Chimp Girl and her orange-green complexion, silky long hair, daisy of a dancer. I'd rather move my feet next to her than eat.

"Thanks for the twirl, Thumbo," she says. "How's that knee?" She's the only one who remembers my knee. She picks me up and squeezes me hard and kisses me warm on my noggin. "Sometimes I wake up like a horse with a broken leg," I say, hoping for more.

Chimp Girl's worried up about Alligator Man. Tells me he can't sweat the way we do and it's killing him. He should be bathing in ice vats, living in Sweden.

"Too warm for him here, Thumbo, with his condition. He itches like a dog and he never sleeps well." She says this as if it explains his surly attitude. As if all of us don't have problems.

* * *

When the Comet operator says it's impossible to get sick from his ride, don't believe him. He also claims Chimp Girl is just some runaway with her hair glued to her body. "Not on your life," I say. "She's the real missing link."

He thinks none of us are honest.

Drunk at two a.m., I'm wandering the fairground thinking all of us should be living in the trees, eating nuts and fruit and grass. How Chimp Girl's holding out for Alligator Man but he's too sulky to get it.

In dreams I'm swallowing fires and Chimp Girl is blowing them out. When I'm awake I'm avoiding all kinds of heat. Boss says next month we'll be traveling with Camel and his wife, a headless princess. Chimp Girl starts crying when I tell her, pulling fleas from her hair. It's as if everything is too much for her now. The pouches in her cheeks appear full, or swollen.

She's been hunting for her Alligator Man all night, but he's nowhere to be found. "Maybe he's found a cool pond to soak in," she says, dabbing her furry nose.

I don't tell her that I've seen him with the new contortionist, playing the itchy bit up. Instead, I hold Chimp Girl's hand and I ask her to help me count the stars in the canvas of summer sky.

"The Big Dipper's bending right over Coney Island. See that sweet ladle?" I say, stroking her furry digits.

GEODE

It was a surprise when Jim announced an old pal called Bob would be visiting. He had spoken of friends from his past, but never had he mentioned this one.

"Bob, Robert? Roberto?"

"Bob."

"Fair enough," Paula said. "What is he like? Would you say he's kind? Funny? Peachy? Merry? Depraved? Perverted?"

Jim wouldn't describe people.

"Bob," he said, "appears to have become prosperous."

The dog padded in and sat near his feet, as if to console him about that.

* * *

Only a few weeks later, retired Bob from Auckland plonked down on the lumpy living room sofa and talked about his awful flight. "Like the sky was full of holes," he said. "Food was so-so. You don't expect that in first class," he said.

Bob was large and puffed on an inhaler. Paula offered vodka.

"Good call," Bob said.

"What are you doing with your time these days?" Jim said.

Bob was a collector of rocks. "Here's why I dig them: You can't ever know what's inside a geode until you crack it open," he said.

Jim glared, as if he'd said something rude.

Bob pulled out a rock from his flight bag. It looked like a dinosaur egg.

"This is a little geode for you both," he said, and he handed it to Paula.

"Aw! Thanks," Paula said.

She held it up to her face to feel the plainness of its skin. Jim glared at Bob. "I hear that in first class, you're offered a geisha for breakfast."

"Hahaha," Bob said, but his cheeks became shrimp pink.

"Gotta take the dog out to pee," Jim said, and left.

* * *

Paula and Bob were alone in the living room. "I'm imagining what's in here," she said. She shook the rock, then pressed it against her ear as if it were a shell. Bob watched. She could feel his eyes on her neck, could feel the warm corner of a tag on the back of her blouse, scraping her skin.

"You'll have to crack it open with a sledgehammer, but carefully," he said.

"I'm glad you've come," she said.

Bob finished his vodka and asked for another. She poured herself one as well.

"Tell me about the wonders of first class," Paula said.

"Everything about it is excellent. Usually. It's probably just what you think."

He looked like a once-in-a-lifetime person, his face fallen down and old but sweet.

"How long since you and Jim have seen each other?" she asked.

"I can't remember," he said. "But I wanted to try again." He shook his large head.

* * *

The fabric tag on the back of Paula's shirt felt painful. She couldn't remember where Jim stashed the scissors. Every time she used them, they disappeared.

"Excuse me," she said to Bob, and walked into the kitchen. Jim kept squirreling away the very objects she needed the most, stashing them in hard-to-reach places so that she'd have to ask him for help. She hunted around and then gave up. She took her shirt off and sawed at the tag with a dull kitchen knife. Standing topless in her kitchen, alone like this, made Paula feel better.

She thought about what it would look like to Bob if he suddenly wandered in for a glass of water. If he did, she'd figure out something to say—or maybe she'd offer him a sweet. He seemed like a man who'd forgive a person for their nakedness while digesting a donut.

And what might she say? She'd say that this had something to do with the hole she had long ago dug herself into. And how she imagined that somewhere inside herself, she still glowed.

ZIGZAG OPENINGS

I was calling to see if he wanted to buy a new DSL package, but like everyone else, he already had an adequate one. His name was Douglas. He told me he was a retired quilt designer and asked me out.

He didn't seem to view the way we met as a negative. He didn't seem to feel that being a middle-aged telemarketer sucked.

"You're just as sweet in person as you are on the phone," Douglas said when we met for real. Though my lips were droopy, I straightened them into a smile and glued them there.

"I'm going to be unemployed soon," I admitted.

I went home and told my husband that an older man seemed to like me.

"Good for him," he said. My husband was mostly packed. I liked singing in the apartment alone, and now I'd be able to do that more often.

* * *

That Tuesday, Douglas and I went to the natural history museum. Inside the museum, I told him I was in the middle of an amicable divorce.

"You're a person with interesting moments," he said, and hugged me softly. "I'd like to take you along with me."

We walked past a model of a giant prehistoric chicken. It was huge, very confused-looking. He took my face in his hands and kissed me. "Consider this oversized chicken," he said. "Do you think he gave up?"

* * *

The next time, I met him at his apartment. That night he taught me how to sew up a wound. I expected something sexy, and here he was slicing little jagged letters into his calves and sewing his skin back together with needle and thread.

I could see, while he pinched the flaps together for stitching, that his skin had once been young. He told me when people lose children, they often feel shell-shocked and lose their bearings.

"Zigzag openings can be stitched," he said.

He handed me some cotton balls to blot my own gashes, which I realized were dripping. The shapes I had carved into my calves were the initials of the few men I had loved before I met my husband. I could remember how it felt to love them. The cotton balls were soft white bombs in my hands.

I kept thinking of our geriatric cat that had run away soon after our boy died. How much I had loved that cat too.

I'd always thought bad luck came in threes. And this was my third date with Douglas. But it was great that he had such skillful fingers. If he hadn't been able to patch me up, right then and there, I might never have believed I was fixable.

MY MOTHER'S MATING CALL

They found my mother. She'd been camping in the jungle with a crazy man. On the phone, Mom described it this way: "My belly's distended, and the whites of my eyes bulge. Honey, I look like shit, but I'm alive." I imagined her jumping up and down with anxiety like her voice, hopping and faltering.

"You were acting like a teenager!" I shouted. "Don't you know better, Mom? You hardly knew him!" Was it my fault she'd run off with a stranger? Because I was living in New York City, thousands of miles away?

I suppose I should have seen it coming. She'd adopted a new ringtone—a hissing mating call—soon after Dad died.

"You flew with some stranger to the jungles of Costa Rica? You didn't tell anyone?"

"You don't know what I felt like."

Now she was sobbing. Her "date"—a psychiatrist who had lost his marbles, quit medicine to become a snake whisperer. She thought maybe a viper killed him. She was alone in the jungle with only one shoe.

"I did my best, sweetie." On their second date, he'd given her a jungle vacation package. "I wanted to show him I had real courage." Dad had called her timid and fearful. "He loves adventure. I don't hold it against him. I just hope he's still alive."

Clearly my mother had a mating call, and men were answering it. She might swallow the next one whole.

THE WORLD IS THE WORLD

There was a hole in Mom's bird-painting kit, and it bled. It bled a lot, all over the floor, when my father's boyfriend Chuck was visiting. Which he did on Christmas, when everything about my family felt flimsy. Sometimes she couldn't stop painting birds.

When it wasn't Christmas, Chuck loved my father from a short distance away, which took a great deal of pressure off of Mom. She called herself a "happy customer." She said she deserved a boyfriend too. "Maybe I'll get one in my stocking this year," she said.

She was upset about my tongue piercing decision. I didn't blame her for being angry, it was a stupid idea because it ruined the spontaneous part of eating food.

"Someone wants attention," Mom said. But she was wrong. It was about my entanglement in badness. My own badness, not my parents'. Of course, Dad was the one who encouraged me to do it. He said, "Your tongue art will become your wild beauty."

Mom hugged me on Christmas when I couldn't swallow food because the hole hurt. She smoothed my hair and said, "We need to head over to The Sauce, and you can have a Coke." My brother was old enough to drink but had testicular cancer and was advised not to drink, but he often said, "The world is the world" and drank anyway.

He was angry and he couldn't hide it on Christmas. He'd pretend to pop Dad and Chuck on their ears, but Chuck would squeal at him like a cartoon pig, which was both disturbing and funny.

Still, when the door opened and Mom's own date walked in, I froze. Mom had a son with cancer. She had a gay husband and a daughter with a tongue stud. Things could pile up. Mom seemed unaware of the bright side of living without a man in her bed.

The dude she landed was not very bright. His name was "Perfecto." He looked like a mole but not in the sweet way one imagines those dumb, unlucky animals. He looked as though blindly asking for applause all the time. He shook my hand and complimented my tongue stud. He said, "I bet you can do amazing things with that accoutrement."

I didn't know what he meant, but later, my brain went crazy imagining. The image of Mom and Perfecto together got stuck in my head, so I put it on pause. I took my brother's hand.

"You are very nice to go drinking with them, to even be with them at all," I said. My brother explained he was just trying to make things okay again, because being a people-pleaser was a difficult habit to break.

THE PLANK

It was wet and cold and miserable, and his dog was fat. Fatter than yesterday. Nobody needed a telescope to see how the dog was over-fed, his snout buried in his own neck.

The captain, biting on his pipe, asked her to take off her bonnet. She removed it, and he inspected her scalp for weaponry.

"Clear," he said.

Then it was time, and she walked up the narrow stairs to the top deck as if to scout for land.

It was darker than before. The captain told her not to imagine escapes or roundtrip tickets.

"Never," she said.

This had something to do with how she made the captain feel things he didn't want to feel. He whispered this to her on his birthday, dancing on deck. She had known it already. She didn't say the right words, should have said, "I am honored." He had the complexion of a root vegetable, rutty and orange. She wished she too were plain. She did not want to make him feel uglier but had done so by being alive.

She explained it to herself as if she could talk it over. She said it to herself in bubbles of thought. This kind of existence never worked for long.

He cradled a sword. "It is time," he said.

Shaking on the plank, she remembered her childhood like a dream she hadn't had in years. She stepped off holding onto that dream. Her last thought was how when people die, they come back as money, something her mother used to say. *If you notice a penny on the ground, it may be someone who used to love you.*

STRANDED SEA MAMMALS

I'm standing on the sidewalk across the street, taking a video of my mother on our roof. Since my brother's drowning last year, Mom worries about stranded sea mammals. She's better when up in her perch, binoculars dangling from her neck.

I point my camera right at Mom as she flaps her arms around spastically, shouting, "Porpoises and whales!" Someone slams a window down, and the dogs on our block begin to howl. Dad runs out of the house, yelling Maria, keep it down! But she stays up there frozen in time, squinting into the sun like a gargoyle.

Mom texts me near sunset. Wants to see the video. I climb up and sit next to her, hook my arm around her shoulders. There's a scent of expectation around her, as if this time, my movies will explain something.

How was your day, Button? she asks. What did you do with yourself? Well, Dad and I washed the dog in the tub, I report. And we have a little more shopping to do.

I've processed the video for her, whitewashed it so her skin appears young. But I have no idea how to get rid of the lines of confusion around her mouth, or how to enhance her watery smile.

"You look great here," I say. She squints at the moving images. "I do look better from this angle!" she whispers, softly like a girl. In the video, I can actually see it's her Grand Canyon apron she's holding up for the whales and porpoises to recognize. My brother gave it to her for her birthday last year. She waves it like a flag.

SKIN

After Nell set Johnny's house on fire, I became a self-appointed only child. She'd be in prison for the rest of her life, but I'd cure cancer. People would soon forget we were sisters.

I discontinued wearing her old shoes. Would change my last name as soon as I came of age.

Dad too had a thing for dangerous heat. Especially in Hawaii, where the sun plays an unsavory character in every scene. Dad never wore sunscreen, and he died from a melanoma after a decade of construction gigs in Maui.

"You burn your skin to a crisp like your father did, baking like a cookie in the sun every day of your adult life, you get what's coming," Mom said. She wore Daddy's slippers as if her feet missed his.

Daddy's mole had resembled a little black dot one day. The next week it looked like a dog, with a long pokey nose. "Nell, Maria, take a look at this speck here," Daddy said. We gathered around his forearm. "Which of our old dogs does this cool-looking mole resemble?"

Back then, Nell and I laughed about the idea of a family like ours, caring about the wrong things, our father avoiding something as silly and simple as a medical appointment. Making a game of life's weirdness.

That was right about when Nell lost her virginity to Johnny. He had been her math tutor, but she told me in private that he was teaching her some unusual calculations. I wished he was teaching me too. She was carrying his fractions, she said, but had lost her calculator.

After Nell burned down Johnny's house wearing Daddy's shoes, using his cigarette lighter, Mom started drinking. She'd come home from her second job, selling opera season tickets over the phone. "Ripping off nice old people," she said. She would sometimes bring home a cancerous-looking man to sit in our living room and smile at us awkwardly. Each one looked too tan, more at risk.

And now Mom was wearing Nell's old shoes, the sexy ones with rhinestone straps I used to borrow. Mom and I were the only ones left standing, but our feet were in confusion, our borders redefined.

IT AIN'T OVER TIL THE
FAT LADY SINGS

"I'm shy," I said.

Back then he said he could make anyone's confidence bloom, especially mine. I said if he ever could really pull this off, it would be his best gag yet. I chalked the failure up to his lack of creativity, but then I remembered I was part of the act.

But sometimes, in the middle of the night, when Chuckles was down there, going for the standing ovations, his act became old. The way it felt to me, he stood between me and the Strong Man. "Now that's a bit of business!" I said about the Strong Man. After that, Chuckles stopped trying to win me over every night. He rested his cherry nose on my stomach and cried about how I had never really loved him.

"Honk if you believe in Jesus," he'd croak, and I'd reach down, honk it twice, make him laugh.

The betrayal didn't happen at first, not when it should've. And later, it wouldn't stop. I loved Chuckles, and I didn't want him looking up at me like that anymore, trying his best but failing to make me sing.

My final act of defiance, of course, was to actually sing my song. I'd been waiting my whole life to do it. One regular night, Chuckles doing his mediocre best, it warbled out of me like breaker waves in Maui. He stood up, as if the alarm clock he'd been waiting for, pretty much forever, had finally gone off. "It's over," he said, love dripping from his chin.

THE HEDGEHOG HOUSE

The house was like an ornate hedgehog when she looked at it from a safe distance. She tried to think of it as a friendly place. Her new husband Roberto had brought her there. His father, a famous architect, had designed it. And now it was the structure she lived in. Additionally, she had become co-owner of Cleopatra, a Pharaoh Hound. The kind of nervous, overbred animal she had grown up mistrusting. Her parents rescued old dogs from kill shelters. These were the sorts of animals that had always made sense to her.

* * *

She found herself walking around outside often, appraising the house from afar. Why didn't it feel special when she was nestled inside it? She reminded herself that the roof was shaped like an endangered animal's back.

Later, she would fondle her husband and cook up a nice pot of soup. Someday she would stop feeling like a pigeon around him. It was time to be happy. Sometimes she thought of how simple her childhood had been. Her parents with a sign over the door of their rental house that said POVERTY IS NO CRIME. So strange that she would never be poor again. She was not the same kind of person as her parents. If you didn't own anything, there was still a lot to lose.

* * *

There were these strange little dark clouds, and they hung directly above the house as if to say, *We're not going away easily.* She wanted to walk outside instead of sitting in the sunken living room, slurping a mug of freshly-picked chamomile flowers. She gawked at a cloud that was shaped like a paw. Their Pharaoh Hound, Cleopatra, had such beautifully sculpted limbs. When she looked at the dog, it felt as if she was staring at a movie star. "Why don't you go for little walk, you seem edgy again," her husband said. His hair was cropped short. He had buttery, youthful skin because the imported face cream he used was made from the mucin of snails.

"It's going to rain," she said.

She thought about it quite often, what a weather wimp she'd become—and then suddenly she wanted to see what the weather was like in Alaska, where she grew up. She googled Anchorage weather. She stared at photos of rain and of women standing in line for soup in a homeless shelter. There were clouds in the sky of her living room. They were on a screen her husband had erected to simulate any type of sky. She could walk out the door and not even say goodbye. If she drove to the airport, she would know how it felt to have everything to lose.

* * *

When she got together with Roberto, he said she was a thing of value to him despite the fact that she had nothing. This made her laugh. "But I have my cat," she said. It was true. The cat's name was Nightshade, and she was black.

"Black kitties scare me, no hard feelings," he said.

"Don't be superstitious," she replied. Men were always intimidated by dark animals. In the same way, they were both lusty and distrustful of her hair because it was long, dark, and curly. Things got stuck in it. After making love to her, lovers would wake up with troubled expressions. It worried them, but they craved it. "I'm glad you feel that I'm someone of value," she said. He smiled. He offered to take her out for a large, sustaining brunch.

"I live in a structure shaped like a hedgehog," he had said. That was funny to her. She thought he was kidding. Things felt nice with him then. He fancied her skinny butt, he said, kicking her ass gently with his pigeon-colored boots.

* * *

When they were courting, she noticed the corduroy of his pants was sticky and lint clung to it. His legs, when she rubbed them, felt like Venus flytraps. He held her hand so tightly it hurt. Moved her hand up and over his excitement. "These are good falconry pants," he said, kissing the bow of her mouth. She hadn't known about his hobby, and it suddenly seemed obvious.

"There is a Japanese hawk called Montu that I want you to meet someday." He winked. She felt excited and sick all at once. It was the first time she slept in his hedgehog home. His ceiling lights had the exquisite, warm glow of kerosene lamps. It felt like she was starring in a movie about a woman in bed with a connoisseur of all living creatures.

She thought about fierce Hollywood actors who might play him. Dennis Hopper, she decided. Then she sensed a shadow over her head. Looked around his house, at the way the light filtered shyly through the lounge, as if protected by rice paper. "I knew you would look good here," he said, looming.

* * *

She grew up with the happy stink of dogs and missed it, wondering if there might be something wrong with Cleopatra, who had no hair and no smell. Roberto had owned Pharaoh Hounds since he was young. "My life has been one long Egyptian dog chain," he said, winking. He had her flea-dipped on a regular basis, even though she was never around other dogs. "It's a good breed for falconry," he said.

She didn't know what that meant, as the dog seemed frightened of conflict. Whenever he raised his voice at her, the dog scooted out of the room. She had yet to accompany Roberto and the dog out to the field. She had yet to see a pigeon savaged to death close-up and personal.

* * *

He asked her again to evaluate exactly how much she liked the house. On a scale of one to ten, please rate it fairly and squarely, he said. She didn't know what to say. She felt as if he was asking her to lie. "Ten and a half," she said and smiled with her lips stretched out. He hugged her, and then he was walking out the door with Cleopatra. "Next time you will come with us," he said. She sort of nodded.

After he left, she sat down and tried to remember a day from her childhood. She was an underslept, itchy child, as her parents didn't have the money for soft bedding. The sheets had sad-looking holes and sharp little threads. And yet she always believed everything was just right.

* * *

She sent Roberto a text message right after her breakfast. Right after stuffing a piece of very buttery organic croissant into her mouth. She thought of Nightshade, who was rescued and adopted by a group of cat-loving nuns, and how she had begged him to let her bring the cat along. She had thought of Nightshade as her child.

I have never been so angry, she typed in a text. She didn't say she was leaving. She couldn't explain that she felt as if she was soaking in brine. That she finally understood that in some way, he was hunting her.

She sat there quietly before sending the text message. A small suitcase of her old clothes next to her legs. She thought about his corduroy pants and wondered if she would eventually miss them. She'd be giving up breakfast oysters, midnight champagne flutes, a sweet nervous dog with no doggyness about her. Would be saying goodbye to his roof shaped like a hedgehog's spine. She sniffled and listened to the childlike sounds her body was making. Was she being impulsive? She sent the text and heard a terrible swoosh.

He texted right back as if he'd been always been waiting for her to break up with him in the rudest possible way.

He texted a goofy emoticon with stars flying out of its eyes. *This is the way you do it?* it said. Next, he texted a photo of Montu. The falcon had pale eyebrows and large dark eyes. *This is what missing you feels like*, he said.

FROM *DAMN SURE RIGHT*
(2011)

HER OWN MUSIC

After her marriage blew up, Jane's therapist suggested she join an "I Am" class, so she could hang out with other shells of their former selves. She attended her first "I Am" workshop, which was really an unorganized support group with dancing afterward. Jane saw that for most of these people, deep into middle age, music had become a functionality balm, a way to get through the next hour. That and pumping Visine into their eyes. One member started with the Visine, and it began a domino effect, nearly choreographed.

Fiercely addicted to their iPods, the "I Am" members shivered or growled when she attempted to converse. Worse, the men who tried to talk to her after the get-together had mange or fleas. They scratched at themselves nervously and stuttered.

When Jane dragged herself home alone, thirty new Facebook friend requests glowed in her inbox. She felt desperate for a smoke, had nothing left. If she were a kid she would smoke oregano and pretend it was grass and it would feel wonderful. Instead, she turned on her own music.

* * *

Jane asked "Tarzan" what he was wearing. He said, "Nothing." She said she was wearing nothing as well, and that her name was Jane.

"Good," he said.

"Let's think about something now," she said.

She told him to imagine they were both in a hot tub, and it was very comfortable and warm. Jane could hear a dog barking through the phone, and clearly the man named Tarzan was chewing an apple or a sandwich. There was the sound of a toilet flushing.

"So, your cock is just floating like a pontoon boat near me," she said. "And then, well . . ."

She waited for him to chime in, to say something about Jane's wet tits gleaming under the full, rising moon or something.

"So, it's just floating and I'm getting very excited and all," Jane said.

She could no longer hear chewing, and the dog had stopped barking. She didn't hear anyone breathing, and for a moment, she worried he may have choked to death.

"You okay?" she asked.

"Yeah, why?" Tarzan said.

"Oh, okay, and so, good," Jane said. She was not naked but didn't need to tell him she was really wearing comfy new pajamas. She needed to cut the tag off the collar, could feel just a tiny scratching itch at the back of her neck, like a flea.

* * *

Jane hired a man from Craigslist named Paul to clean the pool area and remove the bees from the water. She liked Paul's ass, the way his jeans would bunch from all he was bringing. She really needed to commit to eating red tuna sashimi for the next three weeks—lunch and dinner. There were ways to fill days that had nothing to do with fatty food.

There was also a bronze-faced man named Haha; sounded like a joke but wasn't. The man said he'd had a terrible afternoon, and she had given him the opportunity to accompany her for a seaweed salad. She told him it was "on her," and, sipping dragon well tea with him, she asked about the name Haha. He said he had always been a comedian.

Paul was only good at scooping bees, and she couldn't stop wanting to eat seaweed with the dark-skinned funny man.

* * *

At night, after their smoke, nothing would stop Haha's voice, all sucky, from burrowing in and out of her fleshy dream and her unstained kimono. In Jane's dream, she was serving tea to young men with shiny hair. In the real world, Haha's voice lived off the blood he sucked from her shins, calves, and her bottom. A tick can draw blood from a person in an ape suit—so hungry, so smart.

Haha's life kept growing, he had hundreds of friends just a click away. He told Jane he was popular because he said things of importance to people. "That's how you collect friends," he said. "Real followers."

When Jane closed her eyes, telephones appeared. They were the only way to connect—she would dial random numbers and say, "Can you hear me? Do you know who I am?" Once, a seven bloomed on her fingers, and she dialed sevens—got a busy signal. Fives felt hungry, maybe fives ate children, so she avoided them. Eights were delightful though untrustworthy, they used Listerine.

Every number had a little problem, and she didn't have anyone but Haha, the size of a dot. Even in her dream, his part of the story needed work—felt false, unfinished. She blamed herself, lived to please. She used his deodorant, his lotions.

He said, over, and over, "Jane is sexy, but she is a real mess." There was one exit, one way to make him happy.

* * *

A year and one day later, Jane met Bill. He was sunning in the yard next door, must have moved into the rental. She had discovered nettle plants growing and needed to destroy them before things went further.

Jane had developed a little problem with anything new, in general, since Haha vanished. There is always a loyalty factor, they say, like thread hanging from your skirt, or pocket lint. Where does it come from? Jane tried not to drag Haha's scent behind her everywhere she walked, but somehow she had started tripping. Once or twice a day, she would trip on invisible rocks or ruts in the sidewalk—undetectable upon later inspection. She would go back like a detective and stare at the place where she'd tripped to figure out how it could have happened.

Jane's words felt shy. She wanted to say hello across the fence, casually. This man had large dark glasses and a bald head. She walked to the fence, cleared her throat, and said, "Hello there."

He didn't look over. She noticed white wires hanging down from his ears. Sunbathing, listening to music, the new neighbor looked sad, as if he didn't deserve to be spoken to. As though he were nothing more than an apparition.

DAMN SURE RIGHT

The man had come up behind me and locked my arms backward. I could feel his cock or gun against my lower back. He told me if I moved, he'd hurt me, and did I know what that meant? I did know, however I was watching from somewhere else (sort of interested in this, sort of not).

My jaw would not open very well. Two police came and one of them called my boyfriend with his phone. They took a detailed report. When asked, I spit my formal name—blood came out of my mouth, but I was not hurt and didn't know whose blood it was.

There was a witness, an African American woman who had been hiding to protect herself. She had helped me up from the dirty concrete floor, straightened my dress, smoothed my hair down. She told the police she was forty-five years old, employed. She gave them her phone numbers and home address. I felt as if I were watching an actress playing a Good Samaritan in a movie, she was so familiar.

She explained to the police that she had ducked behind a vending cart. She described what she saw him do. She said it was awful, and that he didn't need to do what he did, that I was a petite woman. She told them she had helped me up from the floor so I could stand on my feet. I nodded my head to show them she had. She said, "He didn't need to hurt her, damn sure right."

One of the policemen asked me if I had family nearby. My boyfriend Ian, I tried to say, but it sounded like "oyfenian." I wouldn't go anywhere without him, I said, which sounded like, "ahh wed go widout him."

I wanted to walk up Broadway with Ian, out into the middle of the fine day. I imagined how we would sit at the Greek place, touching. Since I was not compliant with their suggestions for paramedics, they told me I would have to sign a release denying medical transportation. Did I understand?

How quickly Ian arrived, as if he were there exactly the minute he needed to be—and how still he stood nodding his head while the police were talking. I hadn't yet said goodbye to the woman who had helped me. I wanted to talk to her, but I couldn't see her anymore.

Ian thanked the police and took forms from them. He told me he didn't think we should go to a restaurant. "We need to do the right things now," he said. He held my hand tightly, and we walked out of the dim station into the bright afternoon. He hailed a cab even though it was just a few blocks to Roosevelt Hospital.

While Ian filled out admitting forms in the emergency waiting area, I slumped in a chair, watching a plump-lipped weather woman on the waiting room TV. The weather woman looked mildly worried about a tornado, though her forehead didn't wrinkle the way foreheads used to do in the old days. She was moving her arms and hands apart and back together, showing the way a situation with air masses was quickly changing. I hated the way she looked, and couldn't watch.

I said, "Don't leave me" when he got up to go to the men's room. I said it to his empty chair. My slurring words made me feel untidy.

Sometimes now, twenty years later, my husband will enter me from behind, and because I can't see him, I remember Ian—his flannel shirt and the smell of his fear and the things he did that he thought would help.

THE LOBBY

My dad in the suite and the TV on, his wine not chilled as he likes, eyelids already droopy and unforgiving. He wants to play Scrabble with me, it's the thing we do at night, but I want the man sitting alone in the lobby who looked at me with crackling eyes as though he were an eel. When dad finally falls asleep in his bathrobe and shorts, I slide to the red velvet lobby. Eel may be caught between bellboys shifting on their legs, businessmen loosening their ties; if he's gone, I will find him. I can wait all night in the red lobby full of geeks, listening to elevator bells. I can sit and dream about taking everything away from him.

SO I DREW HIM A POODLE

I had to stoop to get in because the doorway was caving. Things didn't look any better inside; books and papers were piled, obscuring solid objects. I was not in the habit of visiting freaks, but his cat was gone and that was all he had. One day I would be sore and old and something I loved would run away and I would hope for a visitor. I told myself this, and tried not to breathe with my nose. He drew me a picture of the cat on a paper shopping bag, said he didn't have a photo. She looked like a mutant, or as though a dog had been lodged in her spine. She was half dog and half cat, kind of like a fox, and I wondered if perhaps he couldn't draw very well, even though everyone in the neighborhood said he was a reclusive painter. "Cute," I said.

"No," he said, "she's beautiful." He went to pour some iced chamomile tea, which smelled like dog shit when he took it out of the mini fridge. Or maybe the refrigerator itself smelled like dog shit. It could have been expensive cheese, blue or raw brie, my mom used to get fancy brie and the whole house smelled like a thing had died.

He said the chamomile herbs would calm me, that I seemed all frazzled, that young people underestimated this herb entirely. To prove something, he broke a tea bag open and sprinkled tiny dry pieces of chamomile flowers in a mug. He told me to hold it right under my nose and sniff it as long as I liked.

Sniffing the dusty crap, my head felt plastic, like it might explode. Nobody knew what to say about my mother and her drinking, and I wanted to mention that as the calm came over me. I wished

Mom was the chamomile sniffing type, but she wasn't. Also, I knew we should refocus on the cat.

"I've always wanted a fox," I said, which felt equally important as the cat, suddenly.

He sighed, and I realized he probably wished he'd not ripped a tea bag for me or invited me in. He was going to die soon, I could tell by his gray skin flaps, so I drew him a poodle.

"That was my dog, Stella," I said. He looked at the picture and his eyes watered and he reached into his pocket and pulled out a cracker.

He seemed so naïve and plantlike, believing in chamomile herbs, not owning a camera, thinking I had a poodle that died. Mom and I lived in an apartment where no animals were allowed. I faced the door and decided to walk before anything worse happened, before I could tell him or he could tell me that everything was really fucked, had always been and would always be so, even a hundred years from now.

THE LANDLORD

I smooth my hair, lean my cheek against the wall to chill. He wrote a note next to the emergency numbers, used the clown magnet, stuck it on the fridge. It said for crying out loud, he's letting me live here cheap, letting me use his car, his CD player, his lotions. It's time. Says he's falling for me, even though I'm a walking disaster. Those words.

I walk out of the bedroom I rent from him. I pay on time. He's lying on the sofa, bare feet hinged over the arm. A dish of cocaine and guest spoons dainty on the coffee table near the fruit bowl. I bend down to tie my shoes, say, "Hey, turn on the Jacuzzi, I'll just run out for cigarettes."

He slices a sleepy-bear smile my way, and my mouth stretches sideways and upward like a circus trick.

THE HAPPIEST MALL IN AMERICA

I'm at the happiest mall in America, in a food court place called Fields of Cheese.

He is ordering the Goatherd. He says, "Everything...but onions."

I smile at him when he turns around. He's way too skinny, like Scott, like every guy I look at now that I'm fishing in the sea for so many fish. Sometimes I get vertigo.

My shoes are written on. My friends do it drunk, and I do it to their shoes too.

He stares at them and says he likes them. I say, "Better ugly," and that opens things up. He starts yapping but all I can think about is what I heard on the news last night—a report about the unlikely illnesses brought on by drought. Like invisible stalkers, disease atoms seize you and kill you while you are doing something innocent like choosing a pizza and flirting. Maybe you never liked choosing anyway, maybe you wish somebody would do it for you, but you are not ready to die. Some people get into total denial, the news anchor said. Biting their split ends and pulling off the ones that feel broken. He didn't say that, I just know.

Someone skinny like this needs a pillar to lean on, so I smile at him as much as I can without looking desperate. He looks pretty bad, with pimpled planets lined up in varied sizes along his chin area.

Scientists say if humans just splashed sex hormones into each other's faces, we'd heal and live like animals again. Our brains are depressed and taking too many meds just trying to hack into our spirits again.

That was Scott, the police said. His brain was already ruined by the time we met him, and then his body. All the boys I like have little bits of Scott somewhere inside them, but I have to search.

Skinny kid tells me he's allergic to onions: white, purple, red, and pearl. He doesn't answer my questions.

Still, I'm all ears, over to his table. He blushes like a girl, and soon I'm saying things real soft. So is he, but his things aren't as interesting—the usual. We're whispering lizards, eating stringy cheese together. This is how things start, I say to myself. His eyes follow my mouth, trace my lips. His symptoms are bad, but I won't tell him. He's not even knowing how much is wrong, every little thing that is and isn't.

POUNDS ACROSS AMERICA

On Tuesday afternoon, I line up with other petite brunette actresses, silently, our eyes underlined with dark liner. When it's my turn to walk onstage, the assistant casting director asks me to smile, inspects my teeth for flaws. She has purple hair, a nose ring, and a T-shirt that says 2ND BUTCH BITCH. She looks me over—back to front to back. Says they'll call if I make the cut.

I work in the fringes of midtown Manhattan on the night shift, which allows me days to audition. My coworkers are mainly out-of-work actors. Our job is calling people who've ordered our diet product from a TV infomercial.

The floor manager creates a sales contest to motivate us, calls it POUNDS ACROSS AMERICA! We're all nervous, fluttering and bullying each other. I pile 3 Musketeers bars next to my coffee. A bite, then a sip, then a call. I wave at Jeremy, who's been on the night shift the last month.

The prize is Broadway show tickets for two. I dial, opening my 3 Musketeers. "Yep?" a tired female voice says.

"Hi. Is this Janet?"

"Depends," she says.

"This is Martha Tiffany with Dr. Feldman's weight loss system! Congratulations, Janet! We've shipped your trial order and you should be receiving it any time!"

"Jingle-jangle-jesus!" says Janet D. Higgins, 190 pounds, in Racine.

"Janet, Dr. Feldman is having us call every customer individually so we can design your unique program. How many pounds do you need to lose?"

I can't help reaching for my 3 Musketeers bar. I hear the pop of a fart from the young recruit behind me.

"Fifty," she says, followed by a puff of air.

"Great. How fast would you like to do that, Janet?" I ask, tonguing the caramel nougat. "Three weeks? Heh! Let's see, I'm just looking at the chart," I say. I turn to see what's happening. Dawn (who started when I did) is doing her shtick for a group in the back, saying "Pee—niss" in a Mickey mouse voice. "Pee-niss, pee-niss, pee-niss!"

Janet screams, "Mommy needs a little timeout too, honey."

"Janet, we're looking at...(here the script suggests to improvise)... two to three to four months if you follow the easy step system!"

I look over at Jeremy, his new haircut. He just did a national soda commercial—knows he's hot. He's rolling a joint under his desk, not really caring if he gets caught.

"I got to try something," Janet says. I hear a child yelling.

"Let me get to the other reason I called...and this has to do with what we just talked about. We care about your success as much as you do, Janet, and we don't want you to have a gap in your continuation—an important concept in weight loss. We're real backed up here, Janet! People are waiting months to receive orders because of the success they're achieving."

The script says WAIT NOW FOR REACTION.

"Oh," she says. "I guess that's good, then. Was your name Martha Tif-ney?"

"Martha Tiffany Reynolds," I say.

I wave at Jeremy near the window grid, flipping me off like he always does. I stick out my tongue and he gives me his rat face. We spent last weekend in bed and he's probably bored already.

Janet tells me in hushed tone that I sound like a super, no B.S. gal. "You do too, sweetheart—we love you here," I say.

She says she's a waitress. Her husband died on the way home from work one and a half years ago, crushed by a semi. She has a toddler named Trevor. He's a handful and needs a good preschool. She hopes to be able to afford one soon.

Sweat is forming under my breasts and pits even though the air conditioning is blasting. I say the last line of the script a bit early, feeling my full bladder, pressing it with my hand to make it worse. "You. Deserve. Success."

She gives me her credit card number, saying "Shit yes!" to the Supreme Success Package (the most expensive).

"I bet you're pretty and thin, Martha Tifney!" she says before she hangs up.

* * *

After work I bring Janet's order sheet home under my shirt. I read off each name as I tear the sheets into bits: Kelly, Nita, Jen, Marla, Iris, Nancy, Janet. They will be mystified when there's no charge on their statements and they receive nothing else.

I take off my clothes and stand naked in front of the bathroom mirror. Look at myself from different angles. The way a casting director would.

LOST AND FOUND

house-painter card

T. looks like the man called "House Painter" on the Dream Date Card my friends and I played when we were twelve. We sit on the cold fire escape. Smoking. Watching the whores curdle and separate.

rat

I bribe T. with a bag of sunflower seeds to come to my loft. A futon, dust mites, overdue plays. Empty shells.

ringtone

One night I make my phone's ring a Medieval Druid Rap. He is acting like those poor fireflies I caught and jarred as a child, though he hasn't lost his flashing eyes. Yet. He wants to die cute. Like River Phoenix. His ice-blue cell phone in his back pocket like folded money.

List:

almond massage oil
almond sunset tea
dark chocolate 80%
dry rhubarb soda

lavender bath oil
musk candles
red light bulb

found memory

What's-his-name took my hand, led me to the bathroom, opened the door and slipped in behind me. The bathroom was dark. "Mari," he said. Through the window I saw file cabinets lined up in black, like widows. It was an office building, the late shift.

how we survived

We made calls, sold diet products. All of us were actors or models. Carla was the token "real person." I hoped she'd invite me to a real house for Thanksgiving. She had a real house, a real husband, and two real kids. I gave her 3 Musketeers during break. I couldn't figure out why she wanted the late shift.

mari

He unzipped. "Mari," he said. His tongue tasted like fruit and tacos. Sweet and sour and rude.

sometimes

I can remember his name. Sometimes it escapes like a bug. He was so tall and stupid. These qualities often came bundled together. He wanted me because I was: a. b. c. but not d.

locked

Outdated things make me sad, like the word "howdy." Inside my life are moments nobody wants to remember. My jaw gets stuck in sleep, by the morning nearly locked, dreaming about the twisting coil cigarette lighter my father had in his car.

benadryl

I answer in case he's decided to come for Thanksgiving. His friend is still asleep. He took too many Benadryls, he says. He knows because he saw the package floating in the kitchen trash.

"Not enough to kill himself," he said. He coughs, says he wants to come see the cats.

dressy beagles

We're sitting on the sofa in the den just a few feet from each other, holding the cats and turning on the laptop.

"Pick," I say.

He types "dressy beagles" into the search bar.

Four guys dressed like soldiers holding Beagles in pre–Civil War southern belle costumes. Bonnets and velvet dresses with leg holes and collar trim. The beagles' faces fall, but the men are smiling.

SHE WANTED A DOG

Her daughter was shy and reclusive. Her husband had wanted a son. Her family seemed downtrodden and anxious. They were a small family of three—fastidious. She thought about the idea of bringing home something furry with hot breath that didn't come with an elaborate set of instructions and warranty options. She pictured her husband and her daughter at the beach with it, throwing it a Frisbee. The agile dog catching it in his mouth and running, running, running. Her family battling their brittle nature, chasing each other on the sand. The three of them laughing over the brown paw prints on the beige rug. They could care less, they would love that dog so much. She could see it in her mind and even smell the dog on her hands.

She also knew she was lying to herself. She remembered how it had been hard on their relationship when she rescued a parakeet during their courtship. He hated knowing the miserable bird was captive in their one-room apartment, watching. Fucking became strange and self-conscious. As predicted, the bird became quiet and lost most of its feathers.

Finally, she gave it to a cab driver out of desperation. They didn't break up, but they never spoke of it again.

JEZUS IN THE BACKSEAT

Tara googled a movie of a naked man standing on a fire pit and not screaming. Smiling. She didn't know how he did it. She googled "man standing on fire and not dying," and she googled "schtick." Nothing came up.

Tara went to bed after that and could not sleep. The next day, she agreed to an arm-wrestling match. She knew Ginny's contests would have been unnecessary if she had a more girlish voice, and that the rest of her would make sense then—her full breasts and wild hair that people said was "kinky." If she could stop trembling when she tried to argue, also.

Maybe it was about having porcelain skin and looking fat in five mirrors out of five. Why did she think her stepdad was watching her put on blue sparkle shadow in the hall mirror when it would take a flood to rise him from the recliner? His one shoe off, his bad foot swollen and raised, the TV remote on his lap. Did he think she would even try to grab it? Tara's mother on the night shift and her makeup case loaded like fishing tackle.

Ginny was acting impressed, because they got picked up in a car that belonged to Jezus's parents. Tara could see the Jezus shit right away, the minute she saw his long hair. The dude said, "Let there be light" when he saw Tara. He was her booby prize. His smile looked like hell on earth. The car smelled like honey and cat food.

Ginny got the one with the Brazilian accent. Christ Almighty asked Tara if she'd ever worn a water bra. Tara said to herself, "Kiddo, kiddo" as she took what he gave her from his hands. She hoped they were clean. Next, his paper lips over her shoulders because he was "impressed" with all he could see.

She let the son of God unhook her land bra. Her wireless bra, she joked, but this guy did not know how to laugh. Mostly they did know how to laugh, but this one was too looney. His hair seemed to come off in her fingers.

He had such low eyes and green shadows on his cheeks. The Brazilian and Ginny were giggling outside of the car and Tara was lying in the backseat. She would do this for all the people in the world who never won contests. She was fine already, a naked waif in God's eyes. Tara said this to herself—and like her mother coming home to a sleeping drunk man in the TV chair early in the morning, she would not grit her teeth.

SCREENPLAYS

Whenever I went into the basement, my eyes found Daddy's boxes full of unpublished stories, stacked neatly in prim rows, as if they were waiting for him to return from a trip. His clothes were in clear plastic bins. I recognized one of his shirts. It was a long-sleeve T-shirt with a dog on it. I could just see the shape of it at the bottom of the bin. Mom couldn't deal with giving them away. I smiled at the boxes and bins, saying in my head:

See you later, alligator . . . see you later
. . . see you later, alligator.

Every morning, Mom's pewter hair made her look ancient. My stepdad's lousy "I'm a man's man" cologne stunk up the bathroom. He worked in insurance and thought he was friends with everyone.

Being a passenger all the way to school in her car was the price of being owned. She would pretend she hadn't been crying. Prattling about this and that. She was clueless about the high-definition TV between us, showing a cheesy black-and-white movie, the kind you only watch in the afternoon when you're sick.

Mom reminded me of those sad-looking leading ladies you catch in noir flicks. Her husband dies, and she remarries a hat-wearing hardass geek played by Fred MacMurray, the kind that gets irritated by everything, especially her kid. She predictably turns into a miserable, bitter character. So does her kid.

* * *

I had an office where I wrote my screenplays. Putting it together every day required patience, but it was worth the effort. I loved the building and the un-building (taking it down before she knocked on my door to say goodnight). Knowing it would be stacked under my bed for the next day. It was always there, waiting, unbreakable. I had cut the cardboard pieces myself and they fit together like a jigsaw puzzle.

Every day after school, I went to work in there. I imported a jar of spaghetti sauce, thick Dutch pretzels, black cherry cola.

I wasn't really sure how I wanted the mother in my screenplay to look, though certainly not old. I wrote the first scene taking place in a beauty salon, the woman's hair being colored a deep mahogany red, her scalp massaged by a stylist. In my mind, I conjured the stylist's face, his attention to detail. The way he'd look at the woman, as if she were important to him. I'm not sure why he'd feel this way about her, but he does.

This stylist becomes her boyfriend. He loves kids, he trains animals. He lives on a ranch. He smells like pine. He cooks omelets and crepes on Sunday mornings. He talks a little and listens a lot. He puts his arm around you only when you invite him to.

After writing this scene, I felt a longing for the stylist. I wanted him to wash my hair and trim it just so. I wanted to know what he really thought about my mother—the way she looked and who she had become. I brushed my hair out smooth, and the motion calmed me.

The fighting that happened every night like clockwork was going on behind Mom's closed door. My stepdad was saying, "You see? You see?"

Mom crying.

I went to say goodnight to Dad's boxes. They were dusty. I said goodnight to them three times—turned circles three times one way, then three times the other. When I closed the door behind me, I heard a very quiet settling, like a sigh. I wasn't sure, but I thought he approved of things.

I put the office away and turned on my sound soother to help me fall asleep. I picked the rainforest setting. Birds were chirping, insects humming. They sounded so real.

VILLA MONTEREY APARTMENT, BURBANK

In California the earth shakes, Ma said yesterday, crossing an invisible line from Nevada into California. She pushed the gas pedal hard and the car almost jumped. I clapped for her.

Today Ma's meeting with a real estate company to ask for a job so I get to stay at Tanya's apartment and swim. Tanya is the beauty in the family—fourteen years older than me. She has a bronzed face, streaked hair, is addicted to the soundtrack from *West Side Story*. Her boyfriend, an actor named Sam, smiles at me. He has dark muscles, swimming shorts, Popeye shoulders stretching out against her avocado shag rug. He just got a part in a TV show.

Can you walk on my back with your little bare feet, honey? Sam asks.

My dad was old and always looked hurt—I'd hurt him by being so little and clumsy. Once he taught me a lesson about it, and I never touched him again. Maybe Sam doesn't know how bad I am.

Tanya won't talk about Dad, she hates him so much, so I pretend I never knew him when I'm with her.

Don't make her do that, Sam! Tanya barks—a hundred years crawling into her voice.

Oh, come on. She's a kid, he says, blowing air.

I don't want to hurt you, I say. He stays quiet, waiting. Stepping on him feels soft and hard, squishy. You win, Tanya says. You both fucking win.

Tanya is so much older than when she left home to become famous a year ago. She walks out swishing a bright red towel behind her. She's going swimming.

A kid can't hurt me, he says.

* * *

In the pool, they don't talk with words, just touch each other's faces bobbing up and down in the deep end. I pretend it's a movie. Seven short palm trees stand in a line behind the pool deck as if waiting for autographs.

Mom once told me smog is invisible once you're in it, and she's right. Everything sparkles in Burbank: the vacancy sign on the apartment building, Sam's neon goggles, the lines of water cascading from my sister's bloodshot eyes.

WEASEL

Kurt's family moved into Crawford's house. The Crawfords are dead and buried in the bone orchard, but the house is still there. Mom says it's rented.

Kissing is Kurt's gift. When his tongue is on hers she decides what his real name is: WEASEL.

She says it to herself, rolls it around in the back of her throat.

They are kissing and feeling each other up under a tree down the block from where she lives. His mouth always has a different flavor—today it's Coke. She's getting hungry from his taste. Her stomach growls, she hopes he can't tell.

Whatever happened to your dog? she asks between wet lips.

Left, Weasel says.

She remembers a mangy mutt dog, wasn't the type you wanted to pet. People said the parents had it put down, that it bit someone.

I really want a puppy, she says.

Not one that pees all over the place, Kurt says, touching her nipple. Those are the wrong type.

She feels the sun on her back, water trickles down her arms. Who knows? She may also be the wrong type.

Old woman out walking her poodle under an umbrella gives them the eye, looks at them sideways. Too long. Sees something and can't look away.

Wait, she tells him.

Woof, woof, he says.

She's sick of worrying about what people think. Pissin' fucker, she says very loudly. Her hands thwap her mouth, and she stares at him.

He laughs. Such words from a pretty bitch. Touches her underneath.

FRECKLES

Loretta, Trina, and Junie were real friends, and their backs were brown as beef jerky. None of them freckled, as mine was. Freckles on my face, my arms, my back. Freckles on my lips, flecks of oil or butter or tomato sauce on my T-shirts. Everywhere I was spotted, defective. Only the dog's eyes followed me, as if I were banana frosting or a dog's version of it.

Not until my fourteenth birthday did an electric switch turn on. Out came the family neck, the swan neck, as though it rose from my birthday cake where it had been sleeping. My eyes became purple, and boys called them "picture windows." Well, not boys, exactly, but one girl did. Junie. It was still a compliment, since Junie was a ballerina and valued physical beauty, especially the neck above all else—she knew what to look for, called herself a slut. She had an unnaturally gravelly voice, as though she'd been smoking for forty years, as though she were half man, and when she laughed, it got worse.

"When I'm thirsty I sound like a guy," she'd brag. One night she slept over with her brown back and her dance bag. I became quiet around bedtime, couldn't think of funny stories. She started looking around my room, all nosy, for something to tease me with. When she crawled under my bed I could see her bellybutton popping, an outie, like a Cheerio.

"Is this your little teddy bear?" she asked. She'd found Ted, my childhood pal—a ripped, stuffed bear with a babyish face—behind the plastic storage boxes. Holding Ted by the neck, Junie was trying to make him squeak like a dog toy. I wanted to ask her advice about how to change my personality, how to become tan without wrinkling up and dying from skin cancer.

Anything felt possible.

I slid next to her so she wouldn't rip Teddy up, kissed her for a long time to save him.

BIRD REFUGE

I spend weekday afternoons at the bird refuge, watching the ducks and geese. Today, I talk to a guy named Mike who I saw here yesterday. He tells me about himself, how he used to work for the zoo, managed the zoo-mobile rides. I loved those as a kid, I tell him. Then we start talking pleasantly about zoo animals and idiotic parents and their smartass kids and we talk on this subject for a surprisingly long time. He is funny and cute—but I'm getting cold, and it's late. The sun is drooping way down toward the ocean.

I slip off my shoes and massage my toes, while he watches. They hurt when I'm angry and upset; my acupuncturist says I hold stress in my toes. "Don't go barefoot here, you can get an infection that will eat your flesh from bird shit," this Mike person says.

He sounds like a guy who is good at knowing that kind of thing, something in his voice like a growl. I feel tipsy from the schnapps.

Mike wears hiking boots, has full, puffy lips, and just one arm. His left sleeve hangs off. I don't look at it directly, just out of the corner of my eye. I try not to notice. He's probably sick of people noticing and pretending not to notice. He probably hates me for my lack of forthrightness.

I put my shoes back on, tie them, say, "That's what I need, my flesh eaten," and he smirks.

The duck nearest to us has only a few tail feathers, looks obscene and naked compared with the rest, and basically stays clear of other ducks. It squawks to tell the others to fuck off. I try to imagine what ungodly trouble could have left a young man like this Mike with one arm and hiking boots.

"Do you drink too much?" Mike asks.

I tell him that I am not drinking, and that I don't. He shakes his head and smiles with cute little gappy teeth. I pull a beer out of my lunch pack and imagine fondling Mike's groin. He skin looks baby animalish, and I want to say something intelligent.

Suddenly, I wonder what he is doing here alone, feeding the ducks. Probably, like a freakish person, he is just acting strange as hell because he's already been labeled by people. Nothing matters, is my guess.

"What happened to the arm?" I ask.

"You are pretty," he says.

He clears his throat and says he'll tell me about it if I meet him here tomorrow, not drunk. A feeling of anger overtakes me, starting with a tingle in my fingers, working its way to my cheeks. Perhaps this man is a creep, just a pervert feeling sorry for himself.

"No promises," I say, walking away, skating through piles of new bird waste.

WHAT THEY WERE NOT

I met up with an older boy I had never seen on the road past the bus stop a few times and we got to joking around. Soon it became every day and he would walk me to school. He would point out how certain parts of nature looked like what they were not. I liked the way my brain bent to meet the things he noticed. He did not need a "formal learning institution," was how he explained it. It sounded right, he was smart as hell. He would stand near the edge of the parking lot like one of the crossing guards and watch me walk into the building.

He was an unusual kind of person, a vegetarian with inner smarts who certain people hated on sight. I had never known a boy with hair like his, puffy and still as a rain cloud. There was a snowbank near my school that looked like a tower of tofu. I remember laughing my head off until he pretended to pee on it. That day I ran ahead.

I imagined him spending nights and mornings at the Shooting Star Hotel, or the Astor, or the Golden Tree lobby areas—reading whatever he could get his hands on, sitting there with his mushroom head. The younger ladies probably liked him, and I wondered what he thought about them. The idea of his toothbrush in a Ziploc baggie made me sad and the roots of my hair would crinkle.

He said he wanted to leave things in better shape than he found them. The day he disappeared, I was looking at the way trees were like shaved carrots, noticing it all. I was better than he had found me perhaps, but I did not forgive him. Every day I saw things more like what they were not. Soon it felt too big—houses were caves in soft sand, dogs were children with hungry smiles.

TEAM

Because people are used to getting what they want from her, the dogs have become a team, she is their leader and even that is a lie. When nobody's around, she trots after them. She used to have a job answering phones, but got to hating people by their voices, disconnecting them. She thinks about small things now: biscuits, leashes, bags. The nervous Lab in her walk group. There is always a story inside a story inside a dog. She wakes up believing all she wants, really, is a man's wet, brown eyes.

DAY OF THE RENAISSANCE FAIR

It's the day of the fair, and my friend Vicky's cousin Kyle is sneaking looks at me, flushing and grinning when I catch him, his teeth spaced far apart and skinny. He wears a shield of armor made of recycled cans. It would have been fine (being gawked at) if it weren't for the odor he carries—a teenage odor I don't feel ready for, maybe a mixture of Nacho Cheese Doritos and Brut cologne.

Vicky loves to laugh behind his back, use him for wheels. *Such a freak-face*, she said once, when we saw him walking downtown alone as usual, unaware that his iPod had slipped, his earbuds dangling down like tendrils. Vicky and I are still content sucking on popsicles instead of what some girls do—which might be making us mean (the repression and stuff).

He's already given us money by paying for parking at the fair, since he drove. It feels like, no matter what he does, he still owes Vicky something. I admire his responsible attitude, his scurrying around to stay out of our way so he won't seem like a parasite. Sometimes I think, "Play dead, why don't you, while your cousin the bitch uses you, practices her diva skills."

"Oh, shit, I didn't bring cash. Kyle, can we have a twenty?" Vicky goes (snorts, wrinkling her pug nose).

"Kyle, dude, we'll buy you the perfect present!" she whimpers, knowing how perky her tits look blooming out of her Renaissance bodice, the fair maiden with rusty lip goop.

Kyle seems suddenly frantic, his left eye twitching, looking this way and that as though a predator were stalking him. His face becomes the color of a fruit medley (shades of purple, whiteheads, pink spots). His sunglasses show a tiny crack near the frame, as if part of him is broken but he doesn't know it.

"Here," he says, handing her a twenty-dollar bill in slow motion, as if any quick movement might ruin something perfect between them. I want to smear him with kisses, yet I follow Vicky into the trashy crowd of fake jugglers, kings, queens, whores, and clowns. I walk to the food palace court and buy a roast turkey leg so I can take my time.

I watch Vicky flirt with a tattooed freak selling leather-bound water bottles so she'll get one free.

Kyle doesn't buy anything, and we don't even try to find "just the right gift" for him. That night, at Vicky's house, I keep waking up, imagining the leather belt I might have bought.

TENDERS

He said to meet him in the Tenders & Muffins at lunchtime, that he couldn't say why, which made as much sense as the fact that cat urine glows under blacklight, which it does. I pulled out my phone to see if he had texted, but he hadn't. My phone looked like the cockpit of a plane, and I understood how to make it do hundreds of wonderful things. It was the only object I loved and trusted.

At lunch, the waitress came over and looked at me hard, as if I'd just been playing with somebody's dick. Women looked at me with anger more than I could understand, I always smiled at them, but people are animals and none of us get why we hate each other.

He sat down and said he was very hungry.

"Thank you, thank you, thank you, thank you for coming here," he said.

"Did you see anyone else from production? Is anyone from production here?" he asked.

I loved his belly, wanted to take off my shoes so I could warm my toes on it.

"Nope," I said. "Nope, nope."

"I'm going to tell you too much now," he said, then signaled the mean-eyed waitress and ordered two Polar Bear sandwiches and one garlic fry plate. "We can share," he said.

"I would like that," I said, wishing I had brought my Emetrol, which makes me feel all cozy and taken care of instead of nauseous and bad.

The urge to pee was knocking, or was it nausea, sometimes it all felt the same. I could see he wanted, no, he needed all my attention.

It was time to say something that would fix him. Why did smells bother me so much?

"How tiny..." he said, looking at my folded hands, his face pinking from hunger, or from lust, or from depression. He knew I went to three meetings a day in three different neighborhoods so I wouldn't have much time for small talk, and this was something we shared. There seemed to be a magnet between us, stuck and pretty. I looked at my hands, and they had veins like my grandmother's hands.

The waitress asked us if we would be ordering dessert. I said we would split a hot fudge sundae with whipped cream and nuts. She smirked and nodded. In the bar I could tell what the movie was, it was the one where people became flies and killed each other.

UNDERNEATH

Her mother said they were starting up again, like in books and movies. The first thing she noticed in California was this: the underside of things often look cramped, like a shellfish inside the opening of a shell. She would never touch snow again. She could watch it in the distance, glinting and winking from the mountains every other year or so. She had jasmine, eucalyptus trees, small butterflies. Smells that overwhelmed her with the feeling of "lucky," though she didn't believe it. If she walked in snow, just once, she might be whole again, the feeling of snow and going from cold to warm inside.

The thrill of pony rides, the quiet of a tourist park in October. The feeling that her father is looking for her, but she can't remember his face. Growing up on the warm beaches, her belly button as open to the world as an eye, watching for trouble. Boys were called "Conch" and "Bong." They rode the waves, and she watched.

She would scream on the weekends, throw shoes at her wall. Her mother's problems itched like dry skin. She sank a wooden leaf, imagining it was her father, and still it floated. Later, trouble had something to do with the light in her walk-in closet, the smoke from patchouli incense holding her still. Music tinted the air with who she was, who she had become. Soon, she would be meeting another boy, not her boyfriend, by the creek at midnight. The honeysuckle flowers would have already bloomed, and she would teach the new boy to suck out drops of honey from the stems. She would show him how to be that gentle, to get the drop to come out just right.

YOU SHOULD KNOW THIS

The first time our parents left me in charge, I was twelve, nearly thirteen, old enough to make sure nothing went wrong. They dressed up in clothes I'd never seen, went to the opera in a flurry, as if escaping from hell.

My little brother, Finn, and I watched two hours of Comedy Central, ate chicken nuggets and thawed peas.

Around eight o'clock, his bedtime, I told him he was adopted. He was six now and should know this, I said.

He grinned, doing the crazy tap-dancing routine mom taught him. Shuffling off to Buffalo.

"Mom said you had to be nice to me," he said.

"Well. Finny, that's what I'm doing."

He loved dancing, as though he had batteries—could do it all day, all night. His feet were on all the time.

"You lie," he said. "You just don't want to be my sister." Finn could be a very unattractive child.

"Don't you think I was there when it happened? Don't you think I helped them pick you?" The phone rang. Neither of us moved to get it. Finn's feet stopped and he stood rock still.

"Why did they pick me?" he asked, his nose starting to drip. He needed a haircut, though he'd just had one. They were trying something girlish with his bangs.

"Because you are both wicked and good," I said.

I went to the kitchen and poured him a glass of milk.

"Your arrival was a blessing to them, Finn," I shouted from the kitchen. It seemed too quiet, though it always did without Mom and Dad fighting. When I was Finn's age, I'd seen them hugging from their door crack. He was squeezing her like a boa constrictor, she was gasping for air, trying to stay alive. They were naked, and I didn't know if I should do something to help, so I stayed and watched the rest.

Back in the living room, it was dark. Neither of us thought of turning on the lights. Finny was walking around the living room like a little bird, following the circular pattern on the braided rug. Perhaps he was thinking back to his birth trauma. His real parents. He sat on the rug, limp as a piece of overcooked pasta. Thinking about what to do next. I studied his shape, the bull's-eye part of the braid hugging him in the dim light.

FROM *BIRD ENVY*
(2014)

CASTING

At the audition, he calls me into his studio, looks me over. When he stands behind me, my fingers stiffen. He orders me to open my mouth, inspects my teeth, says I have an Irish-y, Jewish-y look. Not sure it will work.

He orders me to pose with arms outstretched, measures my waist with his fingers. When he stares at me, I look back into his narrow eyes. At home in bed awake, my nerves sit guard like lions. My hair coils around the last dream.

SECOND VISIT

Dad smoked them, so I wanted to try a cigarette. Mostly my eyes landed on his dumb boots. Hiking made him seem mossy, old and exhausted. I told him I helped Mom with laundry and plucking weeds. I wanted to say I'd taken pictures of her boyfriend from our roof. Dad had thick glasses and birdlike arms. The only thing he looked good doing was smoking. To him we were starting all over again. To me we were treating an infection. He asked me if I ate salmon. I answered I liked it poached and tender. He said he'd been off fishing a lot and would soon retire. I craved what was nestled in my nightstand, a hand-rolled joint. I wanted to free up all of this shitty silence. Can I light it? I asked. He laughed, and I imagined him laid out on a long, white gurney and how part of me would split. He let me strike the match and place his cigarette inside my lips.

BETWEEN THEM

Her apartment was filled with birds. They spoke to her but as birds do, so she could only feel what they said. She lay down on her mattress and imagined the birds between them. How one bird at a time would fly away to somewhere safe. How the shelf of time would be filled with seed. She'd put the wish on a thin slip of paper and let it blow away. How will I ever know what it said? he asked. You won't, she said, because you already know it.

RED CIGARETTES

If someone is married or impossible, I'll hoard images of their shiny smiles. Sometimes I'll spot a man stroking a red cigarette. Nothing bothers me and everything bothers me.

I betray my husband with a dog, by loving a dog—not the way stupid people think, by kissing his glossy ears. I betray my husband by holding the pet rat to my lips and letting her smell them.

VIKING

I tell him he can watch, but he joins in. I wake up imagining him lying next to his wife. He comes here for something wild, our little game. I make him grunt. Later, we'll grill chops. On Thanksgiving he calls me at midnight to say I remind him of an Al Green song, though he can't remember the tune—it's driving him crazy. He's lost his appetite, his scalp itches, he can't sleep. What's happening? he whispers. It's chasing him, he says. I tell him everything will be okay because I remember a few Al Green tunes. I start one, and he joins. Little boxes of metal next to our ears are singing, glowing in the dark.

WORRIES OF THE DUCK

She wishes he were more like the females. He appears like all the other shiny males lying at the lake by day, staring blankly at the sun, dunking his perfect head. At midnight he moans miserably about the turning moon—worries the way tortoises do. Near a long-fallen branch in the shallow spot, she sits on their eggs, urgent and large. He comes and goes all day and night with fancy, fanned-out wings—touching the nest, swimming away.

GULLS

These last few years, I've been haunted by gulls, their firm flight toward ocean. Just great to see them fly to something right. When I turn the radio on, I drive toward the gulls and that feeling of holding it tight. As a teenager I remember holding weed inside my lungs, never letting it out. I like to hold things in. I have these colors and they wake up. To nestle with a man, to hold him in, in that way, someday I won't envy birds.

MOMENTS

We waited for the phone to ring, for money to plump itself up and walk through our door. Moments passed with yarn and crochet hooks. I made hats that never fit, put them away in a trunk filled with board games we didn't play.

I twirled my hair like twine. Mom sat alone on Saturdays, yelled at the television.

That year, even fat boys made me blush. I dreamed about kissing the bubble-cheeked boy who ran around the field.

HAT, BOOT, SCOTTIE

We trusted namelessness, had stopped kissing—our not-yet baby falling out and out again, thin days like paper. Silence had something to do with nice people bringing over egg salad and tortilla chips for luck or else boredom.

A baby who never came to earth yet smiled at minnows, darted around my ankles bubbling hard and burping at this empty home, mad at us for waiting. I called them "Hat," "Boot," "Scottie."

THE WORLD

The door closed and we were away from your mother. As promised, we sampled rum, the stuff your uncle brewed.

I sampled you—you were lying down and I was taste-testing the world. This was confusing, and also not. I was younger than you, younger than this moment, but old enough to enjoy the accordion feel of a curled boy-body unfolding.

OTHERS OF SIMILAR DIMENSION AND NEED

Sitting beside a suffering, hyperventilating zebra (really a horse with stripes) was not new to the women in my family. My mother had experienced it, as had my grandmother and my grandmother's grandmother. Now it was my turn.

"For every pot there is a lid," my mother said before she died. Nobody knew why she said it or why only females cried.

Here it was again, a life-and-death moment in the animal kingdom calling for human compassion. In many ways this experience would be no different than fishing for compliments from a bored husband on weekends. The first time is always the hardest. I could not stop taking pictures with my iPhone of the baby fake-horse—sloshing around as though playing in a small, heart-shaped plastic pool. Lazy. There she was: bold stripes facing up, stripes underlining her upturned nose—too adorable for most people's tastes. A fake horse like her mother at best. I prepared my fists, two of them, rolling up my lacy sleeves and folded fingers ready for emergency triage, the kind needed for the birth of camels, rhinos, zebras (horses with stripes), gazelles, others of similar dimension and need.

INFUSED

Counting backward, sucking, I'd poured my body into jeans like shrink wrap.

Are you comfortable with me? he asked too quickly.

His photo made him look twelve years younger than this.

Still, I liked the tremor in his smile. We were at a restaurant overlooking the beach, the red sun sinking behind the ocean infused with rose hips. Sure, I said.

LOS ANGELES

He remembers me like a Hollywood street dog waiting for him. He remembers us sitting on stone benches. He said I hid behind hats. I remember the creepy lump in his right breast, him trying not to worry about it, touching it often. Asking me to feel it.

Parking lots of bad days followed by respites of good, him driving us all over his yellow city, showing me his favorite buildings, explaining why they were perfect.

One night he called me his psychologist. The way he knelt on our shag carpet, presented Mom with a hand-carved duck from the smelly flea market on Sepulveda, the one we rushed through in search of duck decoys, walking fast while I devoured a large mango without a napkin, mango strings like criminals hiding between my teeth.

ALARM

My boyfriend is acting like fireflies I caught and jarred as a child, though he hasn't lost his flashing, gold eyes. Sometimes he seems almost happy to be with me, lying on his floor mat stretching, moving a brown leg up and down slowly, readying to fly. My hair is falling out. You can see it in the sink, darkening the drain.

FILLMORE STREET

She strides through the city with her Labradoodle to meet a friend.
Later, licking shots of espresso, eyeing men like rivulets going nowhere, or hair in soup—she says it softly: cancer arrived like a jelly-
fish on the beach overnight, invisible but real, though hard to believe.
Here's the number for my intuitive healer, her friend says breath-
lessly. Because honey, let's face it—there is nothing more boring than
death.

RECOGNITION

My mother is afraid and forgetful. When a person is mourning they don't know they are. The best dog should find you, they say, but will it? Inside your neck a man waits to kiss you and maybe a cat sits all day in your little house. Your kid says you are too permissive, and she is taller than you now. When you first met him, there was no recognition. There are kids in the military, and that is why they'll caress a gun, amazed they will die. The moon is chicken-soup yellow.

KNOT

His eyes were green, the rest of his face falling. It was morning again, a planet of mornings. That's why he placed dishes so carefully on the edge, he was broken before slipping. Someone walked in and said hello. I ordered a cappuccino. A man smiled and looked at the chairs. I felt the knot in my voice, hello, hi hi, I was only talking to tell us both we were there.

ON THE SAND

We lie on striped towels at Hendry's Beach. Our bellies love the heat so much we talk about everything.

She still looks like a kid, though her voice is deep. Her skinny legs remind me of a boy's. Breasts have recently sprouted, as if defying some long internal fight. She talks about her dad, how he thinks she's shit now that she's not a track star. How her track coach won't believe she can still win so she can't. Her eyes settle on my almost naked body. I do this to her—make her face hungry, so I run toward the ocean.

NEST

Her car becomes crumbier from each corn muffin. She turns on the radio. Huge machines drive past, a dark cloud on top. Her car was once very nice, but these days, she's sitting in a nest of chips, headed south.

PEAS AND CHEESE

She wakes up loving him but not hard enough. He has dandelion hair. Stars fall and zip between them, they can't stop laughing; she falls asleep curled around him like a comma. He is gay, and often, he reminds her that she deserves better. She nods seriously and then forgets. She suggests dinner. Peas with melted cheese. He lets her do that for him.

SYMPHONY

Starts with the French Horn, sighing alone, warm, angry, soft water-like feet rising undersea, flooding the concert hall, my old shaggy scarf, his knees and the worry for everyone he loves swallowed by cellos, pauses carved out of ruined birthdays and his love like string-section pain in dreams; reruns counted in beats, badly timed coughs. Sitting down, this marriage is standing again, and must rest up, rest, then up and again, up.

FERTILE

She was doing a summer walk with her dog. Restaurants were full, fertile green salads everywhere. Men sat with women and kissed them. Birds flew overhead and made insanely pretty sounds.

AFRICAN BUTTERFLY

You're two hundred miles farther from him and you know it is good, but you could open the door and jump right on a train. Not many kids would but you would. You excel at stunts.

When you step out onto the porch, the mosquito screen reminds you that you're an African butterfly, right before the first white stars. The stepsister twins cry like coordinated fire engines. Everyone needs to know it's possible to undo things. Nobody has to miss him forever.

FROM *THE DOG LOOKS HAPPY*
UPSIDE DOWN
(2016)

ROLLERSKATING, BARKING

On Saturday, my best friend, Lila, invites me to spend the night. I'm trying not to fall asleep on the couch watching *The Late Late Show*, which unfortunately turns out to be some gray and predictable Western, when she finally lets me know the whole story. She'd been walking home alone from school on Thursday, as usual, right along Via Esperanza where we often walk together, when she hears a horn, turns, and this hot guy is staring at her, asking her where is Las Palmas Drive? She points the other way, but he just keeps on smiling a dirty, happy smile.

He probably smiled because, although Lila is only thirteen and a half, she's got lips as blubbery as Angelina Jolie's. She's around five-four and always wears platform shoes. Her hair is the color of dirty lemons, thick and long, slightly wavy. Her eyes are piggy, but nobody seems to care. They are green, like certain marbles that are hard to part with.

"Jesus, so what happens then?" I ask, lighting a cigarette from her mother's pack, fallen onto the smelly carpet. The whole living room reeks of cat pee, and the smell of smoke helps block it out. Lately, I've been getting used to Merit Ultra Lights, Lila's mother's brand. I like the way they make my breath taste. Just this year I've decided I don't like smelling clean.

"Well," Lila continues, with a thirty-second pause for dramatic effect. "Then he says he'd give me a ride home." This she reports like a celebrity. Her lips seem swollen with victory. She has more to tell, and it's waking me up, begging me to pull the rest out.

"So what's his name?" I ask. Whatever it is, I'm going to hate it.

"Perfecto," she giggles. She obviously doesn't remember. All she remembers is that he just turned sixteen and he's given her part of his birthday present. She runs to get her suede purse, which I love, from her bedroom.

As she flies down the hall, her hair bounces off her butt rhythmically. She's graceful. There's something about the way she doesn't make much noise when she runs, or skates, or even when she cries. In fact, I've only seen her cry once, and that was when her little brother fell off an eight-foot wall and she thought he was dead. She knew she would be blamed. But it turned out he was just knocked unconscious.

She's back and is holding something out to me in a toilet paper wad. She opens it carefully, tweezers a tiny hand-rolled joint. Lila and I squeal. I think it makes her horny when we smoke, because we end up running around the front yard, barking at the neighborhood dogs, her idea. We try to get them to bark back, and it works. One of them, my golden retriever, is barking madly from my backyard down the block. I can tell it's him by his hoarse, pitiful bark. Occasionally, he'll actually howl, and that sounds great, like it is finally coming from the right part of his body.

We race around the kitchen, ready-made brownie mix open. Her mother is at her boyfriend's house, so there's no problem. As usual, we eat half of it raw. By the time we're in bed and ready to settle down, I have heartburn. I can't help thinking about the boy, Peter Doyle. White-blond hair, a surfer's grin. I imagine them lying together, digging down inside each other like sand crabs. Lila's breath becomes regular, and I turn away from her. Sometimes I love her and hate her so much, I can't wait for tomorrow.

LIKE A FAMILY

The city is always moving its pinkie to tell me it's alive. One day it smells like steaming artichokes—another day, lapsang souchong tea. My friends, other secretaries, gather on the sunny bench like a bouquet. From a block away it looks as if they are complaining, bending backward and yawning. He never liked them, or even wanted to know them, but now that he's not around, they're what I have.

I live on Carl Street near the park in a room big enough for myself and maybe a ferret, a half block from the express train. I work downtown in an office complex where I keep schedules for three generations of architects. For Christmas they gave me a robot dog and a gift certificate to TravelSmith.

My stomach twists like an earthworm after the rain. I tell myself I won't wait for the phone to ring anymore, but have waited all Saturday morning again. When it rings, I count to three, touch "talk."

"Yo Yo Ma," I say.

Calling me is probably on his "to do" list, which I imagine includes trying on new running shoes in preparation for his next marathon, meeting his training coach in her live/work space, upgrading his phone or his GPS running gizmo, catching up with his ex-wife over dragon well tea. Taking the kids for the weekend so she can play.

"What's new," he asks.

He's lighting up—I can tell because his breathing sounds ragged and doggy. Rain starts drumming on my roof. I look at the ceiling, which seems to be sagging in on itself. It's not my ceiling, so let it crumble.

"I miss you at lunch," I say.

"The world is your oyster," he says. He said the same words when I told him my period was late, very late, and that we had a pink color from it all. Still he said he was moving to London to help raise his elementary school kids. The main thing, he told me, was that his brother would never fire me—I was like family. As long as I remained with the firm. His cheeks looked puffy, like he'd just received Novocain.

"So we're a firmly?" I'd said, blood warming up my face like a space heater that really worked.

He didn't laugh. He never laughs.

On the phone there are silences and delays—words that could have been taken from flash cards. My voice echoes back at me, and I hate the sound of it. I imagine the glow of his cigarette littering London. I hang up and it all comes out.

THEM

You would hate it if you knew how many times I apply lipstick now that you're gone. I'm putting it on, like, every five minutes to get through the next fifteen, though I know they use fish scales to make it, and it's like killing fish to put on lipstick for no reason. Nobody usually sees my champagne-grape-stained lips except myself and two adorable medical professionals.

If I had been a cat you probably would have kept me forever, even with an incurable disease. I think about that every time I clean the litter pan, especially late at night. I clean it too often because it makes the cats love each other more, and also because I can smell how sad I really am in the unpleasant odor of their piss, which I've read glows under black light.

In bed, my eyelids behave like cheap polyester drapes, unable to keep out the light. I wake from dreams about us walking nowhere, covered with butterflies. I can taste you with my feet the way butterflies taste leaves and flowers. Without you here, I notice too much about how the town is changing, new money moving in, teenage girls with their rubbery, flat stomachs. They walk around cold-eyed, like billboards about nothing.

Sometimes, I drive to the Taste It where they use organic bags. As I shop, I try not to gawk at girls' stomachs like I used to try not to stare at perfect front lawns. If I had a flat stomach, and a perfect lawn, and if I were not dying—you might have stayed here on my sofa, drinking beer and burping to mark your territory.

I'm a sloth, it's what we had in common. And the fact that our left eyes feel much more connected to the intuitive parts of our brains than our right eyes do!

Also, the first time we made love, I remember how we talked about the fact that bulls are really color blind, how a red garment has nothing to do with their rightful anger. How just having to cope with a cape being waved at you by some short murderer dressed up like a kid on Halloween would be bad enough.

The young doctor took my pulse this morning, prescribed yoga. He had stubble on his chin, and Teva sandals—like you. This guy, this doctor, made me blush when he said he liked my cockroach tattoo. He walked out to get the nurse, held her hand and brought her in to see it. She had a cute haircut, neon blue eye shadow. She laughed, said random. I told them why cockroaches fascinate me, that they can live for weeks with their heads cut off.

They looked at each other, seemed to connect without touching—as if this were all about them.

GOLDSWACK

He sent her a touch-and-talk parrot, named Goldswack. They still hadn't met in person, though he said he loved her soul, and she said she loved his.

The face of the parrot looked like the face of sex, all beaky and ecstatic and involved with its own satisfaction. She placed it high on top of her dresser, above everything else.

With the captain in mind, she lay down topless and bottomless, thinking about tobacco, pipes, and parrots. Blocking out elliptical machines, hormone patches, and Skinny Cow popsicles. The pattering of new rain put her to sleep for a mid-day nap—and while nothing wonderful slid up or down any particular crevice of her body, when she awoke she felt as though she had been somewhere exotic.

I MARRIED THIS

My husband Gordon looked as though he'd found religion—as though he'd never tasted real food before this beef stew meal at Angie and Bruce's. He appeared to be sucking his teeth after every bite, taking his time, thinking about what he'd sucked, then stabbing a new forkful.

"I have to have this recipe," I said, giggling and poking his calf with the tip of my shoe under the table.

"Jesus, the way the vegetables blend into the meat and the meat blends into the sauce—wow."

Angela's new husband Bruce looked tired and bored. I didn't know him enough to be funny—to be myself.

Their cat, Tuna, was batting the glass door, yowling and laser-beaming her eyes on all of us.

"Spoiled fuckhead cat," Bruce said.

"Right, right," Angela said, staring at her nails, which were down to nubs. "Well, as I told you, geniuses like me make things up."

Her breasts were so newly round and high, she must have had implants. I found my eyes struggling to avoid them, puzzling at how oddly they matched her worn face.

"You made this recipe up?" Gordon said. He leaned forward, his foot tapping thing starting. I could feel the vibration.

"I mean, to be able to create something like this is a gift," I said, trying not to gawk at Tuna batting the glass. The cat had always been fat, we used to joke about his waddle. Tuna was skinny now—stringy.

Bruce cleared his throat. He hooked his arm around Angie's shoulders.

"I married this," he said, kissing her cheek, his lips making the sound of suction you hear opening a sealed jar. She seemed frozen, looking at Tuna through the door.

After marrying Bruce, her son, Frank, was sent to a therapeutic boarding school ("wilderness camp"). She remodeled the bathroom—installed hand-painted Israeli tile in the shower.

* * *

After dinner, Angie and I hand-dried all the bowls so they wouldn't chip. She was slow and thorough, her eyelids heavy. She took each bowl in her arms, tenderly blotting.

"Daria," she said, looking at me in that new way, "I did something very wrong."

She motioned me into the bathroom. Closed and locked the door behind her. I was impressed with the beauty of the tiles and the new shower design. Four people could fit.

"Secret?" she whispered.

"Please," I said, grabbing her hand hard.

"I sent him a shoebox with Pez in it. Hundreds. No dispenser, because he won't need that. Candy isn't allowed, you know. Like sending a knife in a cake." Her hand was cold, and I wished I could warm it.

"People have to do something," I said. "For you, this was the right thing."

Her chin quivered. "But to feel like a criminal for sending him a treat…"

I could hear the men clearing their throats in the dining room.

"Listen to them out there," I said. Her pupils were a shade off from purple. Hugging her, I smoothed her cashmere sweater shoulders. Her implants pressed into my ribs. "You're a great mom," I said.

I unlocked the door and straightened my shirt.

She fixed her face in the mirror, squirted drops in her eyes. Then she smiled at me, or at least, her mouth moved up.

We walked back to the dining room and over to the door, holding hands. She opened it wide. "Tuna! Tuuuuuna!" I put my arm around her shoulder to steady her.

The walls were very close. We waited to hear a rustling nearby, but all I heard were the tight voices of our men, talking quietly about the raccoon problem in the neighborhood.

CALIFORNIA FRUIT

We were transplanted Pennsylvanians who understood the value of fresh fruit. The rental house had lemons, oranges, tangelos, loquats, figs. My mother let me take the bedroom that faced the orchard.

I saw him the second week. It was the middle of summer. He lay on a striped beach towel between our two yards, near the loquat tree. I went outside to say hello. I was not exactly shy, though my voice sounded it. An elaborate coconut scent surrounded him. He smiled and asked me to join him. He was tanning, though his body was already brown.

I went inside for my SPF 50 Coppertone, grabbed a beach towel, and went out to where he lay. I asked what his ancestry was, admiring his black tilted eyes and dark, thick skin.

Sioux, he said. He was one-quarter Native American, one-quarter Spanish, one-quarter French, and one-quarter Norwegian. No surprise that he'd been exotically grafted.

He told me not to put on the sunscreen, offered me his wonderful smelling basking oil instead. He said I was pretty but would fit in better with a really good tan.

I burn quickly from the sun, and Mother had warned me not to try. My dad never told me to be careful about anything, but he was dead now. I knew Mom's voice had gotten too strong.

He told me not to worry about sunburns, assured me that my freckled skin would adapt, just like his. He asked me if I would be interested in meeting him again that night when our parents were asleep.

Climb out a window and you'll make no sound, he whispered, as if there were spies in the loquat tree.

That night I put on my nightgown and went to bed. My skin was stinging and bright red. When I touched it, it turned white for a second, then bright red again. I took two aspirin. I couldn't wait to see him again, under a softer light. I was not too young to understand what this meant.

Under the night sky, he looked as dark as a hazelnut. His eyes were thirsty. We started laughing about nothing, rolling on the ground and grabbing the grass—flicking it at each other.

It's warm tonight, he said, unbuttoning my shirt. He ran his hands over my breasts, my stomach.

What's here? he whispered. He put his finger inside my belly button, and scooped out a small fruit seed. He laughed.

I went crazy eating tangerines today, I said. I was glad it was dark because my face felt hot. It seemed I could not get enough citrus flesh. Juice, he said, moving his fingers inside my jeans and into a place I couldn't believe.

The next night we met again. When we took off our clothes, he stroked my irritated skin curiously, as if offering first aid.

Soon you'll get tan, then brown, then perfect, he said.

What is it with the tan thing? I asked. I really wanted to know.

He flinched and stiffened. My skin got cold.

Bugs, he said, swiping at the air. I realized my family's bad fortune could slip over me like a dark curtain.

We lay silent for a while listening to the sounds of night. I decided to tell him about a friend of mine—a girl I knew, whose father insisted their family move to Alaska. He worked for the telephone company because that was where the money was.

She's never even had a boyfriend, I said. Or fresh fruit, he added, bringing my hands to the place above his thighs. We did things new to me that I'd never forget.

A week later, he disappeared. I found out he'd been visiting his aunt next door. He lived somewhere in Wisconsin. I had been so sure he was a Californian, that meeting his strange expectations meant belonging.

It was our first winter in California—just Mom and I. No cousins, no aunt and uncle, no grandparents to visit. I sent them postcards of my beautiful new land. Pictures of palm trees lined up like chorus girls. Huge waves and white beaches. Bikinied women the color of the dark pine furniture we left back home. My chronic sunburn peeled in tiny pieces like snow.

HUSH

It was the second day of the Palm Springs vacation with my sister Helen and her boyfriend Ron. Helen had already taken ownership of the air-conditioned bedroom complaining of cramps. I was fifteen years younger than Helen, who was nearing thirty. Her bedroom door was locked, and I could hear the AC blasting.

Ron and I watched Animal Planet. He sat on the couch, I sat on the floor. I fanned myself with my sun hat. We laughed at the faces of parrots, the way they looked so confused.

Snack food and juice in the refrigerator. I thought of carrying out napkins, chips and salsa—serving him. I didn't know how to be around men, not having a father or brother. They were usually in need of something and I would never know what. As a child, I might be running around, pouncing. That would be fun—attacking Ron.

That first night, when they fought and I heard Helen call him a bastard and Ron call her a psycho, I slept on the couch where it was fairly calm. Still, I only slept two hours. Mainly, I sat in the living room, drawing my feet. I loved them. They were small, size six.

"I sleep with a snake," I heard Helen say in her low voice. Maybe I misheard.

At home, I slept with the cat.

I thought Ron looked tired, and Helen was taking diet pills again. I imagined her dead—what Mother would say and if we were to somehow die also.

I wanted to sleep next to him. She hated him anyway. The idea went straight into my stomach and pinched. I reached for his beer bottle to sip from. He made a sound of disapproval when I wrapped my lips around it. Said, "Uh oh."

I wanted him to see my new breasts, really nothing else. He would say if they were nice. If they were okay.

"Ready to swim!" I said. This was true. There were tiny beads of sweat on my neck and brow.

"Hey, your sis is probably asleep. That pool sounds good."

I was going swimming, a normal impulse, and Ron could follow. Free country. I had my bikini under my clothes, threw the dress off over my head. He grabbed his towel. Through the door, I could feel his eyes on the parts of my skin that were sunburned and peeling.

"Hush little baby," I said to myself.

Outside, the pool was shimmering, and the world, with Ron trailing behind me, felt overcooked.

SAFARI

I remember how he asked me to sit and talk a bit on their front stairs. The frame of their wonderful house was tall, like a tangerine-skinned three-layer cake. He focused his eyes on my calf, and touched it.

I looked at where his finger was grazing my nylons and making little circles. My nylons had a little run the shape of a neck.

"Poor leg," he said, moving his finger in smaller and smaller circles.

"Nets of hell, be glad you are a dude and your legs are allowed to have air," I said.

"And speaking of 'dudes,' never trust one of us 'dudes' when we are on safari or expedition," he said.

"Oh," I said. I couldn't look at his mouth.

"Because I do see these limping animals just…grazing," he said.

SURROGATE

Todd, her brother's best friend, has been her only buddy for weeks now, and he persuades Kim to join him watching the newlyweds in the house on the corner. On weekends, the newly marrieds fuck in the late mornings. A yellowish meek curtain frames their bedroom window like an invitation. Days have been so boring, humid and long, and looking around for stuff to do, they've run out. Paul has been away at technical camp, gone six weeks, and will fly home tomorrow.

The newlywed woman looks to be about a hundred pounds of extra weight or else pregnant, with cellulite on her thighs and butt. The man has long hair. Plump women like to wear black. Todd and Kim spy from the crook of the plum tree. She has come to enjoy spying, but sometimes says, "Yawn."

This one though, the one they see today, is memorable. The wife gives the husband oral sex, kneeling on the floor as though by a drinking fountain. Todd catches on to what is happening first, says, "Shh!" even though Kim isn't talking, his mouth rounding into a nest.

Watching it makes Kim squeamish, so she watches Todd's mouth and her face gets hot. To quiet her pulse, she thinks about her brother's face, her brother's return. They watch until the end. Then they slide off the tree.

She and Todd have simply run out of things to do. They've played board games and computer games and skateboarded at night.

Today is the day—they'd printed and signed a contract to dash across the train tracks thirty seconds before the train the Sunday before Paul came home. They both like the idea of spicing things up and pissing off Paul when he finds out. Overall humidity is nearing one hundred percent, and Kim says, "We should be wearing goggles and flippers, the air is so wet."

Todd's hair is longer than hers and probably makes his neck hot. He looks like a girl, tall and angular with model-straight gold hair and see-through skin. His eyes are the blue of pool lights. People think Todd and her brother are gay and they are used to it. They even laugh.

Kim knows she is pretty because the boys at school do not talk to her. Todd does, and for this reason, until her brother gets back from music camp, Todd is hers.

She imagines Todd will notice her electric magnetism when she drinks from the Boone's Farm Strawberry Hill bottle. Todd brought a beat-up and rusty corkscrew, and she brought the wine from her brother's closet. Only she coughs when Todd is concentrating on twisting the corkscrew in just right, and the explosive sound, a cough like her mother's, messes things up.

Some cork penetrates the bottle.

"Fuck," he says, and shoves the bottle into his mouth first, gulping loudly, and spits cork like tiny fish.

"What time is it?" he asks. He has a stopwatch, but not a real watch like Kim. She doesn't answer and takes the bottle into her mouth, wrapping her lips and slugging it. It tastes like Robitussin. He's not looking at her, trying to dig something from his pocket. She feels as though she's going to throw up, counts silently with her eyes closed.

Todd rarely smiles. She feels sorry for him because of his massive overbite which has never been corrected. She tries to imagine what Paul will say about the two of them watching sex and then getting a bit drunk and running in front of the train…only she's losing track of why she'd tell. Todd farts and laughs, then makes a "phhht" sound with his tongue and teeth. Kim swallows a few sharp cork bits. Maybe she's never felt so adult.

"Hurry," he says.

They walk briskly to the tracks. It is almost time, almost. He moves in close to her and touches her shoulder, and she is not her brother. He kisses her on the lips quick and dry. As in the movies, she looks up into his face. He promises to run in front of the train right after her, five seconds later, counting loudly.

HELIUM

Carbonated Cat is my favorite drink. It's my sixteenth birthday. This was what Mom and Dad always concocted for my birthdays, this kittie-cocktail. Mom mixes spicy ginger ale with grenadine and adds plenty of tequila to Daniel's drink.

We sit out on the porch and watch the leaves curl under. Mom says we should all toast to me.

Daniel says there is nothing to toast to. Mom is very still.

Daniel says, "Let's toast to the great idea that this young lady may become something someday."

There are sharp, coughing noises from a motorcycle down the block, and further down the block, the old guy screaming to his dog a million times as though the dog were possessed.

I throw my glass and it crashes into the weeds. Mom and I are standing and I tell her in a loud voice what he is—what he did in his car. It is not embarrassing anymore.

He says I am full of hateful lies and what a spoiled little tale-spinner I have become.

Mom is taller than I have ever seen her.

"Get the fuck out of here NOW! And get some help! LEAVE!"

Daniel's face is red and he looks like a fat old man. He can't do much about it since I am calling the police and he knows the neighbors are listening.

He goes inside to pack up and we sit there holding hands, Mom and I, tightly knotted like helium balloons trying to stay here on earth.

QUACK

He tells her this: "When ejaculating, I quack."

"Promise?"

She's poking water next to him—tipping front, then back, and then over again, looking at the sky, sideways.

He gets her feathers moving in such a good way. Shy, yet it does not impair her ability to look directly back, into his bright, bright bill.

She looks away, then straight at his bulging eyes.

He amuses her with whispers of his friend's attempt to corkscrew females with promises of Fritos.

"Fritos," she tells him, "never work with me."

She bubbles, preening her drab brown sweater—terrible next to his bright bill.

As he climbs her, she paddles and slaps water as though she can go somewhere.

Quack!

A middle-aged woman, strolling the pedestrian path with her husband, says, "How come in duck-land the male is so goddamn beautiful?"

Her husband, slight of hair, not quite her height, puts his arm around her.

DESERT AIR

Second day at the summer cottage, my bikini is damp. My hat is hiding, playing an evil game. I pour a little of Mom's Kahlua in a plastic cup, lick the sides. Yesterday I kissed a root-beer-skinned boy who said he'd meet me at the pool today at one o'clock.

My big sister watches perched on the sofa, a sweater over her shoulder, staring at invisible graffiti on my body.

"See ya," I say. She gives me the finger, goes back to her book about time travel.

Outside, the desert air feels fake, like a blow dryer. By the pool my boy looks me over as if I dropped from a tree, as though there were no yesterday. He dives into the pool like the tip of an arrow. A group of girls near him explode in squeals.

THE AGONIZINGLY BEAUTIFUL
NOSES OF NORWEGIANS

Tonight, Albert Albertson took me to a foreign film at the Cinemaclub—a Norwegian film in which ten gorgeous people died. The women had agonizingly beautiful noses. Their deaths were as agonizing as their noses, and it seemed fitting, or at least it fit, and I didn't feel as sad as I would have felt watching normally attractive people die.

The father of one stunning dead Swedish girl had a perfect nose, white-blond hair, a movie hunk, and I mean this guy was like walking sex feeling, the women in the theater needed to suck popcorn when he walked onscreen, his snow-light hair, ultra-kind glasses, and square everything and brewed coffee-colored eyes, probably smelled like male musk. A chin that matched his car. "Hurry," I thought. "Die if you are going to!"

My own father was round and wobbly and had a very ugly car, and died in a quick and explosive heart attack and really that is the way I think it is only fair to go. The date I was seeing the movie with, Albert, had a round nose, three-quarter-moon-shaped ears but maybe they just looked so because of his unusual lack of facial structure, i.e. cheekbones.

The attractive thing about him was his wit, the funniest and only straight guy in my acting class, even his cleavage-shaped belt buckle made me laugh, and the fish on a ladder tattoo on his back, a back I had massaged before the movie, in the middle of which he turned around and started kissing my neck and I said, "I have a neck injury, be careful, and also we're going to miss the movie."

We hailed a cab in the wind, and I felt for a moment that I had betrayed Albert Albertson and was determined to charm him back, I would not reject him again post-movie, I didn't want to reject, it was my New Year's resolution.

In the movie, when Albert grabbed my hand, when his warm sticky and buttery fingers circled mine and he landed my hand on his thigh, I felt anything but wild, a tiny bit betrayed. For a second, I felt I might fall—which made no sense as I was sitting.

Albert had bad breath and my birthday was coming. I could be a grandmother in some cultures, primitive cultures, and my tits would fall and wobble like egg noodles.

IN THIS LIGHT

John does not own a wall mirror. "Sorry," he says. "We can use each other's eyes to know we are human, okay?" He does not believe in reflections.

There are drops of semen on my lips when he says he loves me for the first time, and tears. I do not dry them.

* * *

Twelve hours after my husband David and his bike were destroyed by a truck, people distributed hospital smiles. My cheeks smiled back, bile gathering inside my throat.

Congratulations, you are now a bird with no tree.

They'd thought he was dead, then changed their opinions and had something to say to me when they found me sitting against a wall in the waiting area hallway. He was alive. But not his spine.

"You may have heard it wrong the first time," the hopeless/happy face of the doctor/nurse said. Someone held my hand, my hands.

* * *

David had been home with twenty-four-hour care for just over one year when I started walking alone in the city in the middle of the night. For some reason I felt an urge to buy milk in the middle of the night, which we were never really out of. I was not frightened under any circumstance.

One of the many nights, walking alone in midtown at two a.m., I was held up at gunpoint. A group of youths with hanging jeans swimming around their knees blocked me, squealing, "Who the fuck said that?" They took my money, and one of them poked my nipple. I felt as though I were watching it happen a short, safe block away.

John owned the Ice Mart where I bought the milk. Every night he was there, listening to music on his iPod, talking to the few slumping, tired customers. He always stopped talking when I came in, said, "Hello, nightingale." The night I was held up, John looked at me very hard, but didn't ask what had happened. He offered me Kahlua, and I cried a little. We sipped from the same small bottle—watched each other's lips.

Maybe my cell phone knew something beforehand, because it vibrated often and for no apparent reason.

Now, John vibrates, I vibrate. I crave his lips, his eyebrows, the smell right below his stomach. What it makes my body feel, so stupid, so young.

* * *

David molds delicate cats and birds with colored clay. He can use his fingers very well now.

"His fingers do the walking!" the day nurse says. This nurse, Jill, a handsome and strong girl, has full breasts. David's eyes rest on the window.

Behind his wheelchair, on the wall, a photo of us newly married. Goofy, grinning. Redwood trees. I am wearing the felt hat with the little pink cloth rose. David always said it made me look like Clara Bow.

"Okay, well, I'm off to finish up some stuff at the office and grab some supplies," I say. "David, you take care of this fine girl." Jill is used to this line, nods.

"Sure thing, and David will be very happy to see you tonight," she always says.

I kiss him on the head before I leave. He says, "Aaaah, aaaaah."

His lower body is covered with a thin blanket, and this way, I do not have to see.

WAIST HIGH

"Touch my scar," he says. I do that, with my lips, trace his scar—outline it until he moans. We're toasting each other waist high in the lake, near noon.

Taco laughs, trails off. Under the water, his scar appears the shape of a long tadpole.

Tonight we will drive to Reno, head over the mountains. We both love snow tubing, and we worry for endangered animals.

Kicking the day around, we hold hands, share Jolt Cola. We visit the thrift store off the main road, and I see them.

"I want to get married wearing those shoes," I say, pointing to some slender pumps in the window. I know how they'd feel sliding on. "These are Pink Baby Mouse Skin Shoes!" I gasp.

We check our pockets for bills (I check his, he checks mine, I check his front and back, he is chasing me around the store).

The lady at the cash register says we can have the shoes.

"Take 'em," she says. "And leave."

TOXINS

Irina cut our hair when we lived on the hill. She was a blonde Russian woman who wore pale powder, fake eyelashes, and blue liner. She rented the tiny beauty shop on Polk—two chairs near the window, turned away from the sun.

One cut she told me about her ex—how he left her with no money. Their teenage son was taller than her now and stayed with his girlfriend too often.

Men all want one thing, she said. Even my own damn kid. That time she styled my hair round like a mushroom.

My husband Leif and I were still newlyweds who stacked tofu boxes and refrigerated safflower oil. We lived next to a Chinese beef jerky factory. Toxins floated in our window. All the newspaper stories were about cancer. Skin cancer, throat cancer, pancreatic cancer. We didn't have enough money for furniture, much less cancer.

Leif became irritable the day of his trim. He swore while he was shaving in the morning, cutting himself more than usual.

What's the matter? I asked. She flirts with me, he said. What a bitch, I said.

I imagined him a small child on the beach at Long Island Sound, his mother leaving him alone for a sec while she put on her suit. Something about Leif was unnaturally vulnerable. He had serious asthma most of his life and lived with too much worry.

We went together. When she saw me, her face reddened. I picked up a *Vogue* and sat quietly while she cut his hair.

You two are like a comedy team, she said.

As if to illustrate her point, Leif told her a joke about how much hair he was losing because of my tofu lasagna, my tempeh casserole, the lack of meat in our diet, as if I were poisoning him. I felt my hands get cold, though I tried to fake a chuckle.

Irina laughed so hard she snorted, doubling over as though she were losing urine. She cut his hair deeply, winking at me grotesquely. When we walked out, Leif was nearly bald on one side.

A week later, walking to the health food store, we noticed her windows were taped. A sign in the door said FOR RENT. The shop was dark.

We saw it as somehow our fault, purchased expensive algae tablets from the health food store to fight off cancer. We swallowed bits of ocean each morning before opening the windows.

VEGAN

Beth had glitter makeup that someone gave her. I wondered who. It was still sealed, she'd never opened it, and it was in a small box of unused makeup, stacked with other belongings. I knew she would want me to have it now, so I brushed it over my cheeks and eyelids. It made me look alive, and I smiled at my face in the mirror. It was still my face—a face that was born looking spoiled.

"Don't ever talk to me about boys or meat," Beth said on her last birthday.

"You mean men?" I asked.

Beth forgot we were grown up a lot. Nothing mattered as much as the fact that she couldn't find any size twos and I was trying to help on the Internet. When we were little, her hair smelled like teriyaki chicken. I remember telling her as though it were the highest compliment. She pulled my arm so hard I never wanted chicken again.

"How would you like to be fried?" she said. She was a vegetarian, a vegan, and eventually bones and skin.

The doctor said it was not because of her diet, it was her brain making her body die, and then it finally did its job. One stupid nurse said that to my mother, about her brain being in charge. Mom turned to the chair Dad would have sat in, and said, "See?"

IN THE SHALLOWS

The darkness was in early now. She said she looked like a Holstein with her black and white jacket. Men walked by and smiled at me, not her.

Her jacket was playful and spotted and she was overweight, so yes, I suppose she looked a bit bovine—but in a nice way. She spoke often of her double chin. It didn't bother me. We were friends. We always walked around the lake, every day toward evening, rain or shine.

I could smell Kahlua in the air, maybe just the holidays nearing.

A scribble of rain came down and skittered the walkway, pimpled the man-made lake. The mile loop around it would soon be slick with silvery leaves from the young trees.

"Are you afraid of lightning? Or do you love it?" she asked.

I never talked about my man or about anything that had changed for the better. Secretly, my bed had become a home again. A place to live.

My man-friend didn't like her, said, "She sounds cruel."

"No, you don't know her," I told him. I should not tell him anything about her, but I was starting to.

* * *

On our walk, she stopped at the place where a huge oak had fallen in the last rainstorm. The roots, she said, smelled just exactly like her husband. She said, "I smelled him, just before they hauled the tree carcass away."

Her husband died in a car, and after that she had gotten heavy. She'd become a mottled thing.

I thought about men, how many there were, but how none of them would likely thrive with her again.

NEEDLES

Forgiveness is everything, the acupuncturist tells me. He says I have toxic rage—that's why I get so many bladder infections. Jabs eighteen needles in my arms and legs.

At the hospital, my hand is warm enough to touch Mom's cheek without her flinching. The doctors and nurses don't know I dance at The Sauce, smile at me with respect. Not Mom. That's why she's dying. If she could talk, it wouldn't be better.

Before I leave, I tell her the story she told me when I was a kid, about the old castle everybody forgot about because it was so dilapidated. A princess lived there but nobody knew. She sang inside the curling walls, the stones that tilted.

Later, after the show, a bulbous man in a black Mercedes says he'll pay for a photo. Just you and me, he says. When he puts his arm around me, I'm still sweating from the lights. I look like a Martian in the gold tassels and pointy hat without the other girls dancing near me. I can tell he cuts his own bangs.

CASH REGISTER TAPE GIRL

Her job was driving from gas station to gas station, selling specialty cash register tape with ad space on the back. She sold it to the mini-mart managers. Ads like "FREE WASH WITH ANY FILL!" printed on the back of cash register tape, the stuff you always threw out.

She knew how to smile well because she was an actress. She had been studying acting since she was ten years old. She had been to an acting conservatory. She knew how to smile, but her eyes grew tired anyway. She practiced in the mirror, throwing the cash register tape in loops like a lasso. The trick was to position the tape around a gas station owner's shoulders, to get them touching it, eager for what came next.

Back at her office, she slunk into her cubicle, added numbers. She touched her hair, it felt slick and hard. She was close to winning the highest sales award of the month. She was preparing for an interview with an agent in a few weeks and everything might change. She just needed more money to buy some clothes, so she didn't look all washed up when she went places.

* * *

One of the gas station owners was Sammy. He had two beagles and a wife who was living somewhere else. They had an open thing. Sammy had the worst breath she had ever smelled, and it made her wonder if he were ill.

They went to a violent movie in an IMAX theatre. He ate an

extra-large buttered popcorn, but she wasn't hungry. In the theater, she got a headache and it made her shake.

Later, he drove up Mulholland, didn't look at her or speak. He stopped on the side of the road early in the morning and fell asleep while she watched him snore.

To him, she was a cash register tape girl.

She thought about Nina, a role she had played in Chekhov's "The Seagull," the world of Russia a hundred years ago. The life of a young woman losing her mind.

MAYBE

I notice the short guy loitering in places that make no sense; churches, abandoned running tracks, parking areas—banging his backpack against a hip.

I see him near the bookstore, a place to stay dry from the rain. Later, I will say to him that he has a MAYBE stuck to his face. He will say that his face doesn't know what it is saying.

There is nobody home. He touches my hair, as if he is here. I say, "Hey, there is nobody else here," to the dog. But I smell him. Somebody is really touching my hair.

I am smoking again. It is getting worse. Women here discuss dog food ingredients and how many calories it takes to eat a carrot versus how many calories are in the carrot itself. They talk about which actors they think are hot and which actresses they think are sluts. They haven't said more than "hey" to me, it seems. I may not be here at all, which is comforting. Their earrings are so cheap they don't know how to smile.

I live alone but I have the dog who looks sad when he's right-side up. Best to try and get him to roll. I wake up to sun and weeds, a canopy of TV talk, the loud neighbor's SUV and once again no milk, no eggs.

Anyway, the short guy may be married. Or else, this could be his day, he may crave a beer and ask me to accompany him and I will do so. That's what townies think a woman like me would do, and I'd hate to disappoint them.

My husband Ezra used the word "frigid." That word died in the last century, I told him. Ezra died in this century. Now my body is the opposite of frigid, it is horribly alive.

The short guy asks me if I drive a car. He can't, he's too short. Bad idea, he says. For sure I say. No driving and drinking.

We have a few beers at my house, then whiskey. We do what living people do. Afterward, he falls asleep on the dog's chair.

Lying on his back, gazing at the ceiling with wet eyes, the dog looks so happy upside down.

THE BIG DIPPER

The pool was four feet deep, and we bought it at Target half off. You could float on your back and think, "Fun times are here," because at least you weren't burning hot.

Mom and I watched it fill up with hose water. She looked around at the backyard, the neglected fruit trees, and said, "I've got to call those idiots and make sure they get a gardener." It stunk from rotting fruit and dog poop.

I wasn't going to worry about anything. I would just float on my back in my bikini. I would be weightless. There was an annoying flea bite in the crook of my arm, which I sucked on.

The pool was going to be my way of making more friends. I was sick of the two friends I had from last year. Lila and Blythe were both considered to be strange. Lila wasn't ugly when she washed and brushed her long hair—about once a week. She memorized animal facts. Blythe looked like Pinocchio. She was a violin prodigy. Had a European haircut—short, black, severe. She was proud of her breasts, which were large, adult size. I didn't have any breasts yet, but the doctor said not to worry.

I wanted to know if late development meant small breasts. Mom said it didn't, that she had been the same way. "Worth the wait," she'd say with an exaggerated wink. Now that Dad had his own place and his bipolar disorder, she had all kinds of new expressions.

In my new pool, I would float on my back when it was dark, looking at the stars. Nighttime swimming had been my dream.

Since there was no one else, I invited Lila and Blythe for a nighttime dip on Saturday. Lila couldn't come because her family needed to drive to Oxnard. Blythe said she sure as heck would be able to make it. She was all about nighttime and pools and stargazing.

"Show me the Big Dipper," Blythe said. "I want to make sure you know which one it is."

Blythe was wearing her bikini bottoms, but she left her top on the side of the pool. The pool seemed much smaller with her beside me. I was glad it was cheap. Terribly absent were Lila's cigarettes.

I pointed to the area of the sky where I saw the Big Dipper.

"Uh huh," she said. "A long, bent ladle, right?"

Blythe looked wet and slick, her womanly breasts gleaming. I felt angry at her for taking her top off.

"It looks like a crooked dick," I said. The pool was a bee cemetery. I scooped two up and threw them out. "I don't even really know what a ladle looks like," I added.

I could hear all the neighborhood dogs talking to each other. A bee might have been marching down my arm. Something tickled.

"You know what a crooked dick looks like?" Blythe said. Her face was large, or maybe it was the moon.

"Not exactly," I said, trying not to let my eyes get caught on her nipples, "but I've seen them, and they all have different shapes."

True. I had a subscription to *Playgirl*. My mother had given it to me for Christmas instead of a new bike. Once she'd found a beat-up copy of *The Happy Hooker* under my pillow. I'd stolen it from a garage sale. When I came home from school, I found it laid out on my dresser next to my hairbrush and retainer case. Nothing seemed to freak her, as long as she had two martinis.

"So, like…whose?" Blythe asked.

"I haven't seen that many dicks, I just have…" If I told her I had a subscription to *Playgirl* she'd tell Lila, and then God knew what would happen when I stopped being their friend. The water in the pool was getting cooler, the smell of new plastic making things worse. I hoped she hadn't peed in the pool, though I would not put it past her. "I have a lot of cousins," I said.

She smiled at me so brightly then, she almost looked pretty. She squealed, half laugh, half death cry. She said she was getting cold—hey, what a great idea, let's bake oatmeal cookies.

Suddenly she said, "Could you imagine sucking one of those?"

"God, no," I said, fast and soft. Her eyes looked back at me big, full of thought. She moved in.

"What do you imagine they taste like?" I knew better than to speak. "Corn on the cob," she whispered into my ear, spitting, "with a bit of salt."

This was not happy news. I knew that violin prodigies lived exotic lives, they were much older than other teenagers. They traveled to Europe.

I imagined Blythe kneeling in front of an audience, her mouth open like a baby bird.

"I'm not ever going to do that," I said. It sounded fake, as if I were acting in a play.

Blythe moved to the far side of the pool. The moving water sounded smooth. She kept still, cupping her chin in her hands. I wondered if our friendship was done.

Her nose was cartoonishly off-kilter, as if a person had sculpted the middle of her face blindfolded. She practiced three hours a day after school, was going to be on CD covers wearing velvet dresses. She was going to be rich. She already knew everything that was going to happen.

FROM *CELLULOSE PAJAMAS*,
PROSE POEMS
(2016)

CELLULOSE PAJAMAS

I consult a nutritionist who believes in dark greens: collards, kale, chard. Hope blows in like swallows nudging the window ledge. I wash the dark green leaves carefully, softly, just for him. We will share them on the drive to the grocery store, wrap ourselves in their cool cellulose pajamas, tell each other in bird language again and again how it was we grew too close.

SCRAPS

Ma says stand back while she strikes the match, lighting the Wedge-wood stove. There is an end-of-the-world whoosh as gas and flame mate—omelets out of scraps are keen, she says, sucking a Menthol, arranging button mushrooms as eyes, red onion slices into tight little smiles. At dinner, my sister's hair hangs like a thick curtain around her face. Sometimes I'll poke through it, whispering, how much for your last three bites? A dollar, she'll say. Ma can even make a piece of cooked cow look lovely, we both agree, trying to raise two children on her own. My sister excuses herself for the bathroom after dinner. Mom and I look at each other as the sink hisses, then the angry toilet joins the music. We pass the time by inventing situations, playing two truths and a lie.

GUEST STAR

Rain is starting. My sister stands next to her groom, and next to the rabbi, exotic animal, her special guest star. The groom, hawk handsome, is shelter. The yard is protected by a huge palm, a fig tree sprouting out between its roots. Guests are cooing unanimously, as if roosting. I'm nineteen, slouching, holding a wilting bouquet. My mother and I feel light, as if drunk, as if we could lean forward forever and not fall. In the air, the good luck smell of wet grass.

NITE, MONKEY

"Nite, Monkey!" he said. Rain grabbed my window, settled as dust. My father, the world explorer, back from a mission of taking pictures, sneaking into ruins, his face a crumpled map: streets, volcanoes, wind. God told me about you, I said. He laughed, told me the truth—world travelers search until they drop. His eyes sizzled like fat. I followed him anyway—to slums and secret meetings, to hear his laugh, to understand his game of secrets.

EMERALD

He asked her to choose a shade of green. He liked the way she stooped to tie her shoes like an old man, as though she could fall over very easily.

Go! he said.

The window was open and she screamed it. He asked again.

BIG SISTER

The night my first period started, my sister and I were watching the movie *Harvey* and we laughed.

Her hair seemed heavy on her shoulders, a long, thick curtain.

I peered through whenever I could to catch a glimpse of her strong cheekbones moving.

Later that night, she told me about an adventure she had with a man until I fell asleep.

When I woke up, I snuck into the living room and found her there talking to the cat.

The cat was laughing.

LAST CAUSE

Tonight I ate crackers with guilt instead of cheese, thought about my cousin who is round as Weeble. I see gum on the sidewalk, ignore it, I know assholes and he is not one. He is tender, tucks it under his umbrella, his mind can taste it. Let's say there is no successful love poem. I compare this to a strike of the heart toward the very last cause, maybe the only bird born that round and soft, so much beauty nobody knows what the fuck to call it, what kind of bird it is.

RUBY

I nibble popcorn while the movie burns through my body. I'm his ruby-throated hummingbird, fighting to be still though quivery when he says it, he says, *Suck the popcorn, my girl, take time with it in your mouth, each salty buttery piece as I will you, and I will let you fly.*

SALTY

It was when she loved a man with eyes like a fishbowl that everything changed. With his kisses she would swallow clear water. Fear would rest behind colored pebbles, be gone for entire seconds—long enough to bubble inside and out. I love this, she spit, swallowing his air, his name, dancing backward with it on her lips.

PRIMPING

In the photo he looks ragged, fierce, wears a bandana. He lives with his father, up north. I am thirteen, rushing from mirror to mirror, removing childhood by applying blue eye shadow, black eyeliner. I stare for half an hour at the perfect rings around my eyes.

Mom is out selling houses. I am alone, baking cookies, imagining him on a beach. I sculpt the raw dough and roll it out, just right.

NURSE

The fourth month, one of her tricks was being his nurse. She'd bring a towel and put it on his forehead. She noticed he preferred pencils to pens, made shopping lists, Please, please buy these things! the lists would say at the very top. Q-tips for paintbrushes. Homemade paint from coffee grounds. He painted birds, mainly. Honey, she'd say, this is better than anything.

Please, she said, teach me.

CLIMBING OUT

I wake at dawn when he bangs his mini gong. His mouth wide, lips so flexible they could swallow a rabbit. I'm afraid to jinx anything, climbing out of his futon. "Talk is breaking many rules, but listening is holy," he said last night when he sawed me in half but didn't. I listen to him listening. The city smells salty. Orange light sneaks around his shower-curtained window, cabs call like geese, or mothers of missing children.

SINGING

He didn't allow my mother to sing, but once she tried, with me on her lap.

I remember the forbidden sound of her voice, the way it trembled like snow on the tips of my ears.

She thought he was relaxing, taking an herb bath. He was a doctor and needed his sanity.

He ran out of the bathroom yelling *Stop singing*! smelling just like the holidays.

DR. V

My foot is darker than the ocean. It's turning blue—he promises to stop the pain, and I picture him in a world of shark eggs, he rolls them toward me like unbreakable promises and there is nothing to do but keep them. When he calls to say there is one more option he sounds tired, blue gauze covers his telephone voice. I want to soothe him, but that's not my role. Twitching fish, bones and blue cartilage, I can't help shivering as he casts his needle between my toes.

WIDOWER

She sleeps at his apartment once a month and warms his hands between her thighs. Her open, shell-shaped mouth kisses his closed
lips. Her tongue, only once, tried to pry them open.

"Otter," he calls her, knotting her hair with his knuckles.

An otter is just an otter.

People say he howled for months after his wife drowned. Then
he went and rescued incurable, difficult dogs. The neighbors were
embarrassed by the whole thing; the limping dogs, the howling.

THE NEW

In the morning, when she opened one eye, his face was above hers.

You look like a turtle, he said.

Half asleep, she felt a surrounding shell. In her dream about him he was a spotted owl, peering around the meadow ready to choose which mouse had caused the trouble.

Turtle, he whispered, stroking her hair.

Kissing her awake.

FROM *ALLIGATORS AT NIGHT*
(2018)

ALLIGATORS AT NIGHT

You remember when you lived in Florida briefly, walking to the store with your husband in the middle of the night. You remember the sound of alligators crooning like deranged, nocturnal cows, all the way to the 7-Eleven, from each side of the highway. You remember thinking they must regularly sing to people on their way to the 7-Eleven—mostly a welcome sound, because there is the three-hour walk there, and the three-hour walk home, and the night sky is so velvety in the summer, and the singing alligators are like jazz. It's like you're in a jazz club, but walking, outside.

Walking to the 7-Eleven, what you sometimes want is to never actually get there. Because you are holding hands, feeling his warm, fine skin. He has not yet had his dose of whiskey and his breath has not yet become thick as a mushroom cloud. You have not yet said you have a migraine and that you don't really feel like snuggling because your body is so sweaty after the six-hour walk. You have not yet cried or threatened to leave and you have not yet been quieted by your husband with his body half-asleep and given up the fight.

You remember that your walk to the 7-Eleven is glorious, you are both present but so quiet, the two of you loving the sound of strange overgrown creatures who are so close to you, but attached to their watery homes. Sometimes you imagine these animals are chasing you and your husband all the way to the 7-Eleven, but mostly you just think of them there in the dark, without alcohol and probably without love.

SEPARATION

My husband is reading on the bed. After packing, I find myself staring at his penis, which pokes out the side of his shorts. It is friendly-looking. I will miss it.

"You are staring," he says.

"Yep."

"Still leaving tonight?" he asks.

My stomach is rotted out from too much coffee. He gets out of bed, grabs at a Kleenex box behind the bookcase. His clamshell mouth closed and round.

The telephone rings.

Four miscarriages in the last two years. Each time we adopted a rescue animal. One of them, the gray tiger cat, is dozing on the foot of the bed.

"I am, but. . ."

"Remove Zelda," he says.

I pick her up and take her to the sunny living room.

On the bed, when I come back in, his shorts are off—not his shirt. His right hand is already moving evenly, tenderly. He seems to want me to watch, is gazing at me with a tiny smile, so I unbutton my shirt for him. His sperm is rising, hopeful and stupid.

The room smells like fresh bread.

SEX IN SIBERIA

My imaginary man lives in Siberia. We touch down on each other like helicopters. I smile, move my mouth around him—offer a warming hut, a place to explode. When he bursts, storm clouds open.

Southern California boasts mild, featureless people. The Weather Channel's talking heads, all botoxed and baby-fatted in their cheeks, ramble on about radical snowstorms in New York State. I paint leaves, collect Styrofoam in buckets. Driving downtown for wrapping paper, I count the fake blonds wearing two-dollar Santa Claus hats.

My parents divorced and nobody yells anymore, but that is no longer important. I want a Siberian life, a Siberian husband. One whose hair changes from brown to light.

My dog seems worried, so he and I take long walks. Sweat trickles down my back. The dog pants miserably. I promise him someday we'll skate alongside a large man who loves Labs.

In December, I slump into bed early, imagine what it will be like—Siberian sex. Better than any other kind—so cold outside, so warm under the covers. I ball up socks and rub them where the man would go. We're there, and he is teaching me how to taste snow.

BAKING

Gathering in the living room for wine on Christmas Eve—coughing, moving chairs at commercials. I would have started baking three days ago, Mom says, in a monotone.

At the stove, I'm already scorching the second batch, remembering the tune Rick made up, the way he whistled it naked. Cookie sheet's warped; sifter's missing a handle. Puppy trips Mom near the bathroom. Jesus, she hoots. Can't someone do something with this dog?

I drive to 7-Eleven to buy more flour, puppy in my lap. On his cell, Rick says his manic brother showed up—spun a web in the corner of the living room. His mother's crying and drinking after a year dry.

Merry Christmas, I say.

You too.

He tells me we should get married, move to Mexico, become Buddhists.

Buddhists, I say, inhaling puppy's breath in the cold car, snow falling like rice.

THERAPY CAT

It was not a snub. The therapy cat he brought on our second date, sitting like a bodyguard on his lap at Zito's Pasteria. Me showing sufficient cleavage, he with his therapy cat, called Uma Thurman.

"This is useful, for all of us. We all need a bit of it," he said.

I agreed. However, I hadn't known (I explained) that there was such a creature. I knew about therapy dogs, of course. But not cats.

"Oh yes," he said, with his thick, boyish hair. "They're growing in acceptance."

The cat was white and very round. I found myself feeling a bit less than romantic, leaning forward and attempting to be even the tiniest bit showy. She owned his lap. Her back arched, but so did mine. She was probably fixed. So was I.

"The goodness of a therapy animal ripples," he said. I agreed. I used to have a husband. In a way, he was my therapy animal, until we stopped being good for one another. Good for the soul is good for everyone, of course.

We ordered crab. The cat looked angry. In spy movies, cats are diabolical animals, as cold and murderous as their owners. This was never true. "This is my second date in the last thirty-five years."

I nodded. It was my fifteenth date since my divorce, a date that was obviously going nowhere. He had lost his wife. She died. He said they never really dated, he and his wife. "Nah. We just hit it off, and that was that." He stroked Uma Thurman, therapy cat. "Uma knows," he said.

"So listen. Let's not look at this as a date at all," I suggested. He looked at me as if to say something, then readjusted the way the cat was sitting on his lap.

"Yes, well, there is a lot of bacon in the world. It all smells great but then you find out what it does to your heart."

I imagined how frisky a man like this could be without all of the scar tissue.

"May I pet her?" I asked.

"Of course you can," he said.

I knew I'd never date him again, and there was something nice about petting an animal when one felt very sad.

ALBINO

We went to a thrift store and joked about trying on hats and getting lice.

"Miami Lice," he said.

Was he safe? I hoped not.

Was it scummy and frivolous to hang out? I hoped so.

My birthstone was emerald. I told him, and his chlorinated eyes said, "Well, that makes you not-simpleminded."

We both laughed. An albino laugh. Watery veins stood out, and his forehead looked like a stolen woodpile.

I wanted to make him butter from real cream. I wanted him to tell me all about the Stone Age. I wanted to know about what they did without butter, how they licked fire. How did he become allergic to garlic and light? If he had never been outside, and if they studied his condition in universities—he was one in a million.

Anyway, that was part of the dreamworld I lived in at that time. If he existed, he is now elderly, or dead. Most of the time I don't believe in him, or the curative properties of green tea, or a stern-assed God.

OUR WOMAN

This week our woman hobbles around the house wearing fluffy, taped-together slippers. It appears as if she has broken a toe. Last week, she was a braying like a donkey, and the week before that, she appeared in the living room, wearing a wimple and praying. We feel lucky she has chosen our home to be stuck in, and we roll with her changing ideas of herself.

Since the woman has moved in, I notice how our walls are the color of stomach medicine and that our lighting fixtures are unsightly—one of them has no shade, it's just a bulb, which dangles from the ceiling like a goose. In the bedroom, an economy-model light fixture so weak she claims she can't find her socks. We have very little energy to change things with the stunted woman around. Sometimes she'll pretend to be blind and gather her socks with her eyes closed. Indeed very amusing, we laugh. We know our house needs help.

I guess you could say she is a very unusual guest. Nobody really asks us why she is here, or when she's planning to leave. Each week offers a new kind of entertainment. I wonder if stringing fairy lights around the hobbled woman's waist would be a fun idea, but I haven't asked. Not yet. When she moves in permanently, we might make her into a functional Christmas display. This is what I am thinking. Perhaps it isn't very realistic.

WE WAS SWEET

We had dinner that night at a rathole, a Godforsaken grill, a place we had tried to avoid and had done successfully for thirty years. We would have to celebrate our thirtieth wedding anniversary at Vito's. This anniversary should have been a festive occasion for any couple, but even more for people who have not touched the other in twenty years of a productive, thirty-year union.

First thing in the morning, we shook hands, high-fived, and said, "Yay!" I cleared my sinuses, and Bob performed nasal irrigation with his neti pot. We wanted to feel ready for a celebration of family values. We was sweet. Underlying the mean newspapers lived an angel with nails of pearl. We were both quite nearsighted.

"Well," said Bob. "This calls for a bit of meat!"

This meant that Bob and I would settle for dinner at the squat brick steakhouse—the only place in town NOT full of pole dancers from the annual conference and workshop here. Slim women with five-inch, spiky heels, in town again, holding hands, with menstrual concerns. Around the city they clip-clopped.

We walked to Vito's because we didn't have a car. We were the opposite of negligent. Long ago, we had a broken car which we sold to our washer and dryer repairman. He never spoke to us again.

THE BUG MAN

Ma often said that despite everything, we were lucky people, because the Bug Man came over to our house for free, sprayed in places nobody had ever seen. Places we never knew were there.

Happy times were when the Bug Man pulled up, in his strange truck with a giant plastic model spider glued to the top.

"Your mother means business," he said to Josh and me, blinking into the sunlight.

"You're one lucky dog," he said to Muttsy.

Once, when he came to spray, he hugged Ma in the side yard. They seemed to want privacy. I watched them from the upstairs bathroom window. Ma looked pretty in his long skinny arms, like a different mother.

I thought maybe our lives could change. He could marry us, become our father, and take us to live in a large, bugless house.

But three days before Christmas, Ma, reading the newspaper, slammed down her coffee cup. It splattered the table, dripped onto the floor.

"Ma, are you okay?"

She sat mesmerized, glaring at the newspaper. I grabbed a roll of paper towels to clean up the brown puddle at her feet.

"Cancer, just like his father who started the goddamn pest company!" Tears rolled quickly down her nose. "He's already gone," she said, sobbing.

I hated the word. "Cancer." She looked bitter and ugly saying it, as though it was stuck between her front teeth. Josh ran outside, good at acting like nothing was wrong.

Watching her cry, my ankles itched. They were already covered with flea bites. Soon, families of spiders would bubble up through the floorboards.

I cut out the Bug Man's obituary, as if he had belonged to us.

TEETH

He handed her a plastic box filled with his childhood teeth. At first she thought they were a gift. In a way, they were.

"Oh gosh." She picked one up, rolled it between her thumb and index finger. It was tiny.

"This is sweetish," she said. "Your mother kept these until now?"

"Isn't it great?" he asked.

"Yes, it is, it really is," she said. His mother had kept them in a plastic box, he said. Far away from heat for forty years.

Thinking about this created a briny feeling in her mouth. She imagined him a little boy so often these days. Laughing too carefully, throwing the world off.

How he would have looked back then, trying not to lose his teeth.

DOWAGER'S HUMP

Sometime in my forty-fifth year on this very planet, one night, over dinner, my husband would examine my dowager's hump with squeezed eyes. He would clear his throat and suggest I needed to see an osteopath.

"How long has that been there, honey? Aren't you about thirty years too young for that kind of thing?"

Our son would ask him to pass the salt and pepper shakers. "This meat is very dry," he'd say.

My husband would inquire about the spicing I used to baste the chicken we were eating. Was it fresh thyme, or dried? Organic? He'd suggest it tasted a bit too spicy, or not spicy enough. He'd suspect it was overdone.

"Well, that is my little secret," I'd say, patting my hump.

"Maybe you would not have married me if I'd told you about the family problem?" I said, once, very softly.

My husband would twist his torso away from me, right there, in his chair.

My hump, like the moon, would rise a bit higher.

Sometimes, doing dishes, my mother's hump, my grandmother's hump, would feel very close. I'd find myself in the lobby of some new-age healer's office, trying to explain.

One day a doctor would come out of his office and shake my hand.

My son would be next to me, then, showing his plastic boa constrictor to the doctor, squeezing it with his hand. He'd say it had a mom-hump already, but nobody could recognize it yet.

CUTLERY

I knew exactly what he meant, so I wrote my lover a letter in which I told him that I was getting good advice, finally, and that I needn't return. I knew he was without Internet and accepted that he would never receive my message.

I asked him how things were going with his cutlery collection. He would duck into a kitchen store for hours. Catalogs did not work for him, it had to do with weight and feel.

"They have lots of ideas," he said after leaving a kitchen store, smiling like a child at Christmas.

I had read articles about the way Chinese beetles mated. I'd watched videos of rattlesnakes having sex. We were each part of an intricate and delicate habitat, and we had our own ways of surviving. He had his butter knives. I had my fantasies of finding a man who would find me.

BENEFITS OF KRILL OIL

My pharmacist smells like the old Wonder Bread factory, and though forbidden to smoke, he does. If I were dying, I'd break the rules too.

Across the street from Duncan's pharmacy where I work is a fancy new organic food market. I try not to shop there, it's crazy expensive, but I'll admit to being taken with a long-haired cashier who doesn't remember my face.

"You, young lady, go and have some goddamned fun this weekend," Duncan instructs. But I don't like leaving the shop before he does these days. Sometimes he forgets to lock up. Anyway, I don't have fun at night—unless my Cuban neighbors invite me over.

* * *

Walking along the sidewalk to market, there are tiny beads of herbicide in the cracks. But no one walks.

"Spencer the Magnificent, I'll bet you don't remember my name again," I say, standing in front of the cashier, holding my lunch which is, once again, red tuna sushi. Once, I asked him if he was from Florida. He wasn't.

"Yes I do," he says.

"Then what is it?"

He stands there, hands on hips, flipping his long hair behind his shoulders, pressing a finger against his full upper lip, as if thinking.

"But my whole family is this way! We all suck!"

"No worries," I say. I remind him that my name is Polly and that

I work right across the road, at the tiny, antiquated pharmacy. I tell him Duncan has lung cancer and soon the pharmacy will be gone. I need to become more memorable to him, and quickly.

"Someone will probably turn it into a doggie nail salon," I say. Spencer does not seem to think this is amusing. Maybe he has no sense of humor.

I've become fond of red tuna rolls and tofu chocolate pie and will miss buying them daily. Spencer will continue checking out women's balanced meals and herbal cures. He will smile at them and say, "Excellent choice." He will remember their names.

I look down at my bracelet, hanging loose. I've been reducing since Duncan let me know about his condition. Nearly a size zero, even my arms have dwindled. I never want to work anywhere else.

It will soon be my birthday, and to celebrate I will talk to the checker about the health benefits of krill oil.

"I am not a whale," I'll say. "I don't understand why krill oil would be good for me."

Maybe this will amuse him. I'll shock him when he sees me buying two slices of tofu chocolate pie.

At the window that faces the market, I can see Spencer talking animatedly with a new, pretty employee. She resembles a Golden Doodle, created to appear a certain way. Her corkscrew curls are angelic, but phony. She doesn't even create a shadow on the asphalt.

Even from here I can see Spencer's cheeks have turned pink. Perhaps he's shy around women he really likes. I tell myself that when he ages, he'll look like a rooster.

Someday, this period of time when I worked for a dying pharmacist will be a weird memory. It will have very little significance to me, but I'll remember the way my boss cared about me and how young the cashier across the street made me feel. A feeling like that is hard to replicate. Nobody really knows why good people disappear.

WOULDN'T YOU LIKE SOME SUN?

When I asked Mike why he was always walking around the house naked, he told me he had too much to hide. That was the year his mother sat on the train tracks, and the same year his brother fell in love with small two-seater planes. The kind that break when they hit birds.

Also, Mike had lost his job and refused to send out resumes. He said there was only so much anyone could do, he was sick of worrying, and when someone wanted him, they would holler.

I'd gotten so used to Mike's nudity that I'd stopped noticing his penis crouched like a worried squirrel. I'd started feeling nauseous about meat and could no longer eat chicken. There was something about all of his skin, all at once, blending with the smell of olive oil on salad. Also, the scent of dope made it hard to notice anything good or warm about the house anymore. Always, there was a drawn shade.

"Don't you want some sun?" I'd ask.

"No, goof," he'd say. "I want some privacy, can't you tell?"

"Sure," I'd say.

Once, I said, "I bet if you wore clothes, sometimes you would be able to have really good privacy."

A day later, he left. When I got back from the vegetable market, his note said, "Jim and I are testing his two-seater plane and I'll be gone a few weeks. Take care."

One of our dogs was blind but very affectionate. She slept in the bed with me, right where Mike had. Moon was nicer than Mike had become, and she had silky hair. She'd gaze into my eyes and steel my resolve to keep things clean, hairless. I held her, imagining Mike and Jim skimming over the edges or else the tips of buildings, trying not to die. Laughing and almost letting themselves crash. Looking into each other's bursting, purple eyes.

* * *

Mike called from Nevada. My guess was Las Vegas. He said he was in a tiny town called Primm. I pictured his worried squirrel. I imagined he was finally warm.

"Oh, wow. So how is the plane doing?" I asked.

"Oh, good, really good. We are really really really doing good."

"No plane crashes?"

"Nope, I'm good! I'm in one solid piece!"

Then I heard a sound which grew to fill up the holes inside the phone. Heated up metal. A woman's laugh. A giggle, to be specific. "Piece?" the voice said, tittering.

My lips made sounds while my body caved in like a paper airplane stabbing the wall, the floor.

* * *

I was not the kind of person who liked to go out—but now, all I wanted was to be free of the house. I drove from coffee house to coffee house. I tried out every customer bathroom. I learned the name of the guy who made the best lattes in town. Jerome. Girls lined up waiting for their lattes, and stuck their tits up. I had never seen so much tit thrusting or hair swooshing. Jerome was sweet-looking, with a curled upper lip and stubble. Dark curls, like a Caravaggio. Cute as a colt, young and easygoing. The kind of guy you'd like to bring to a restaurant and have people wonder if he is your young lover, your toy boy.

And yet, Jerome seemed to enjoy eye contact with me. Sometimes I thought it was my imagination. Other times I felt like his girl. I would stand in line and not stick my tits out. I left my tits just as they were. I would, however, apply cruelty-free lipstick before entering the coffee place. I was shy like a teenager again; with Mike gone, I felt like a kid. I blushed when he called my name.

"Latte for Jean Veevee!" I would not correct him. I couldn't.

And then, one day, I did.

"Genevieve," I said.

"Huh?"

"Genevieve?"

"Oh fuck," he said. His face pinked like a cooked shrimp.

"No, no! It's fine. I just, well, I come in here a lot, and I thought I should tell you."

"I am a clod," he said. "That is such a rockin' name!"

I smiled at him, and he smiled back. Maybe he liked older women. Cougars. Perhaps I met cougar standards. I did have nice hair, and my skin was nearly unwrinkled due to a lifelong struggle with agoraphobia. When one never goes anywhere, the sun can do little damage.

HABITATS

I go to the zoo on weekends and watch the other visitors to see how disturbed they are. There, you can see where a human is not thriving. For example, a father seems to have his hand glued to his son's scalp, as though the boy is walking away from him. A woman whose swollen eyes look as though she's been up all night crying stands staring at the giraffe enclosure for hours.

When I was younger, I used to enjoy going to the zoo to see the animals.

On a date with the man named Frank, I let him know that I recently bought a "Zoo-You" seasonal pass. I pull it out of my wallet and hold it up proudly to show him.

"Nice," he says. "I like zoos too."

"Why do you like them?" I ask.

"We're a curious species," he says, quickly brushing his shoulder, which seems to be his habit.

He passes me a plate with two chocolate cookies on it and looks at my eyes. I look back at his. His eyes are not exceptional. I can't even tell what color they are. My late husband's eyes were magnificent, the way they tilted slightly upward. At this age, eye color fades. That is because we can no longer reproduce, and nature no longer intends for us to look attractive.

Zoos are surely not the best topic of conversation on a first date, but the damage is done.

While savoring his cookie, my date says, "Can I tell you something funny about my ex?"

"Of course you can," I say.

"She couldn't stand clutter. Even if I was keeping a family heir-loom. If it wasn't useful, she'd take it to the city dump. I was losing my mind. She was ready to throw me out, too."

"What strange behavior!"

"As if that was the worst of it," he says, staring glassy-eyed at his coffee.

"Ah, hey, let's talk of happier things," I suggest.

At this point, I doubt that either of us are good for much more than moving our mouths around, talking about what went wrong.

Outside the coffee shop, wind is whistling, garbage flying. I can't imagine what we'll do after this, but I wish this wasn't a date, that we knew each other well, that we were going home to a warm apart-ment to watch something on the television or to read on the sofa. My brain keeps racing ahead, trying to make me believe I'm still a healthy animal.

BARISTA

That night, it was just me and the barista. Everyone else was finally gone. He was standing in the middle of the social area, waiting for the world to quiet down so he could serve me properly. I stood right next to him at his invisible espresso bar, holding his hand in the wilting light.

Earlier, I was worried about the teenager. I heard her on the phone with her mother. "No, no, no! You aren't hearing me! I'm not staying here over fucking, fucking Christmas!"

And then she cried. Christmas had most of us by the neck. She slammed her not-smart phone onto the floor, a sad little crazy thing, so I asked her if she wanted a cup of something. "Espresso," she said.

"A shot for the young lady," I said to the barista. In a way, she belonged to all of us.

He looked like a confused nurse, as if it was time for treatment, but he'd forgotten who to treat. "Tell your family that it wasn't so bad here?" he said.

Somehow, the barista heard one of us was going to be released. "Must be you," he said. This was right, I was scheduled, but I wasn't sure I wanted out.

"Tell them about the drinks I made you," he said. "Promise."

Holiday cards were being taped to the wall near the TV by a nurse I had never seen before.

"I have to die here for everyone," he said. He said this every day. I had gotten used to him saying it.

I looked at the teenager. She sat on the floor, her arms protecting herself. Soon, she'd walk around the social area asking everyone if they found her to be physically beautiful. Each and every one of us would tell her that we did.

ROUND WOMEN

The women were large as human snails and round as moons. They lolled in and asked my husband for money. He did not know them but I had a feeling he would be nice to them—they were women, and they had breasts.

Between the two round women and myself, there were five breasts in the room, and one fake breast. The fake breast was an implant. I had named her "Iris." Iris is a beautiful name, the name of a blonde woman running through a field of flowers, barefoot.

The two plump women moved in so close I could smell their shampoo. One of the women said to my husband that her breasts were as round as money. How much money would he pay her to touch them? My husband looked at me like a naughty dog might look at its master.

"Would you like to start?" the rounder woman said.

I realized she did not see me there, in the room, with my lovely false breast and my less-lovely real breast. The real breast did not have a name, which suddenly felt unfair.

The other woman (less round) slid off her jeans. She didn't even ask if it would be okay. She had long legs. My husband's Adam's apple moved. He looked like a little boy lost in a huge grocery store. I found myself enjoying the fact that the round women had eye problems and could not see me standing there right in front of everything.

If I really wanted to speak to them, I could. I could even say, "Go away now, ladies, this fella is married," but there was no reason to. I wanted to watch. To see if he could perform under such conditions.

I nudged his foot with my index finger and he flicked it off like lint. I touched his hair, whispered, "It is getting so long now…" and he shuddered. The other woman was watching, taking notes. The rounder woman with the kissing problem kept going.

My husband's eyes were fixed on the window. This made me sad, as though he were looking for me but couldn't find me.

YOU AND YOUR
MIDDLE-AGED CAT

When you return to Yvette's house, she and her friend Uma are drinking wine, cooing over a brochure of eye makeup shades. Yvette's friend looks at you as if something is amiss. "You look cute today," she says, slicing her eyes up at you. "Is that a new shade of lipstick?"

You're relieved. For a second, you wondered if you had bird shit in your hair.

You have recently started renting a room in Yvette's house following your divorce. Perhaps things were a bit too normal before you and your problems landed here. It's very clear that she and Uma have been talking about you while you were walking from block to block, posting notices in hopes of finding a good home for the cat. You don't have a place to live anymore, can't keep her.

"I was just saying to your roommate here, it's too bad I can't personally adopt Snowball," the friend says. She looks you over with her pale gaze. A window is open and there is a smell of fallen leaves.

"But I just can't," she says. "We already have a cat. Her name is Sofa...we'd have to rename your kitty Ottoman to match."

You sit on the floor, making your face neutral.

"I guess my jokes aren't up to par, as they say."

Five people have been on the verge of adopting Snowball and have backed out at the last minute. A husband said no, a kid developed an allergy, and three other potential adopters didn't respond to your calls and emails.

You would never want this rude person to adopt your cat. You have no idea why she thinks you'd want that.

"Why isn't your ex-husband able to keep her?" she says.

Yvette must have told her that your ex has a more stable life, a well-paying job, a lease—but he took to disliking the cat, because she reminded him of you.

You hold yourself back. Yvette looks worried, pours another glass.

"Sorry, I'm really not in a very good mood," you say. The room feels close. You wish there were more open windows. The friends go back to swooning over eye shadow colors.

You walk back into your rented bedroom. It's small, with a rocking chair and a reading lamp. You sit in the chair, remembering the day, six years ago, you and your husband rescued Snowball from a shelter. How she looked like a cat from another century. Round and lush, creamy white. She walked right over and smelled your lips, as if she already loved you.

PLAYING THE CHICKEN

The acting teacher, Dante, has cast me as a chicken in the final yearly production. This makes me feel lumpy, short, and invisible. Playing a chicken feels like being disliked.

He casts blonde, giggly Melinda for the leading role. The kids he casts for the better roles are the ones who squeal when he walks into class, and they all happen to have light hair. I have dark hair and a curved nose.

Melinda is the most motivated. She has started jumping up and grabbing his ponytail, thrusting out her nonexistent tits and narrowing her pool-blue eyes.

I try to hide my disappointment but I feel myself sulking.

"This character is not just a chicken," Dante says. "It is a counterintuitive symbol of hope."

When acting class first started, I loved Dante. He was nice to me. He'd lift me up and plop me down and lift me up again because I was so light.

But, these days, he'll ask how my big sister's film acting career is going. I don't understand the details he wants. He'll ask for the name of her agent, and I'll shrug, feeling my face redden.

"Tell her I'm her biggest fan," Dante says.

* * *

My sister says I should not have to play a chicken at all—and that even though pink feathers may look attractive on me and bring out my skin tone, it is ultimately unfair.

"Symbol of hope, my ass," my sister says. She tells me to stand up to Dante, to refuse.

* * *

At the first readthrough, I tell Dante my sister says hi to him, and that she thinks I should play a human, even if the human is a village idiot or a gnome.

He says, "I'll tell you what. Invite her here to watch the next rehearsal, and we'll figure something out together. Maybe she'll teach us some stuff."

When I ask her, she says, "No fucking way, this is bribery."

I love it when she says fuck. She says it often and I like to sing it in my head. Last year I was kicked out of girl scouts for saying that perfect word.

I keep imagining how and when I will say it to Dante. I remind my sister that a chicken has a past and lots of motivation. I test to see if it will soften her stance. I tell my sister it will be a fun challenge, even though I really don't think so.

She says, "Of course. And you'll do great. But fuck him anyway."

Mom doesn't notice anything, as usual. She's working three jobs now and can't be bothered. She does not sleep and she hates the world for warming up, hates it for all of its crazy-ass problems. She doesn't seem to think me being cast as a chicken is good, bad, or worth worrying about. I believe she is right. Anyway, I'm telling myself I will be a marvelous chicken.

SHOULDER BIRD

This new patient was an eccentric, there was no question. She was nuts, but in a pleasant way. Her nuttiness involved an imaginary shoulder bird. The bird always came with her.

"Polly likes a good warm shoulder," she said.

His late wife had always wanted a parakeet but had never owned one. The doctor didn't approve of domesticated birds as pets.

She was not talking to the doctor, really. Cooing and gurgling, she said, "Polly is a very pretty pet." She, the patient, was lovely in the paper robe, flat against the examining table.

Inside the doctor's mouth, his words felt stuck. Something was gooey in his esophagus. What would he say, anyway?

She prattled on while he prepared to examine her. "Feet in stirrups, now," he said.

"Polly no wanna," she reported to the doctor after he inserted the speculum. A routine exam, of course, but nothing had ever felt less routine, with the bird there.

He really felt the presence of that tiny, talkative spirit. Animals were not allowed inside the medical building.

"What is your favorite hobby?" she asked the doctor while he looked inside. "Polly wants to know. We want to know something about you, both of us do," the patient said.

"I'm a falconer," he answered. He had no idea why he said it. It was a lie. He was not a falconer, but sometimes he felt like one. He could be one. Nobody was going to make him feel badly about the things he wanted to do. Nobody was holding him down or trying to domesticate him.

EXTINCTION

"Honeybees are dying because of atmospheric electromagnetic radiation," she says.

She says this while she rubs his back. Then she kisses the hair below his neck, where it comes to a point between his shoulder blades like a heart.

"What happens in the world, and across the street exactly?" he says, fidgeting.

She can feel him stiffening, and she is going to wait, but not forever, not too long. An asteroid could hit, is likely to hit any minute. The Big One, the nine-pointer on the San Andreas fault is looming like an angry landlord.

"Feed me immediately," he whispers. "Feed me for I am God. I am the Internet."

"I will call you Wiki," she says.

"Did you see the update? There is a gunman with lips pointing toward a man's waist." She kisses his waist, and he knots his fingers deep into her hair.

Species dying every two seconds. Breast cancer multiplying and dividing and running triathlons—making women hate their own lovely breasts and praying for male children so they won't have breasts to poke and worry about and the ozone ripping apart and melanomas on white cats' faces.

She rests her head on his thighs. He lips her nipples, licks them. She moans a bit.

She is a dangerous person, a person who has been treading on the flagstones of men with wives and kids…but this does not stop her from wanting.

GUARDING THE HEART

Since our one and only dog, Donald Sutherland, died, I attend meetings. My husband refuses to join me. That's alright. Some of them are entertaining, so I don't mind going alone.

Last meeting, a man handed me a picture of his daughter's dead Madagascar hissing cockroach. He smiled at me in a secret kind of way.

"We called her Fluff."

I almost smiled back. I could not imagine caring about a cockroach, even an exotic one. But human nature is strange, and one must guard the heart.

Lately, I find my eyes landing on the faces of a few male mourners, amazed by their nobility.

A woman with curly hair and an inexplicable purple umbrella hat stands up and sighs. She explains her Irish Setter was a confidante stronger than her father.

"Yes!" an attractive middle-aged man shouts.

I had a less-than-sympathetic father once. I wanted to shout "Yes!" also.

Another symptom of emotional pain: removing my wedding ring before meetings, burying it in the pocket of my gym bag.

Donald Sutherland died of old age, but looked so young. The day he died, he could have passed for a puppy.

I tell my husband about how helpful the meetings are.

"Shit! Absolute bullshit!" This from a man who never swore before Donald Sutherland died. Now he's critical of everything I do.

Mourning a beloved pet can do this to regular people, quietly. They may lose a sense of scale—and sometimes, a sense of decency.

I'll never bring home another pet. It would kill him.

ALL BEASTS ARE PEOPLE

Gunning it up the hill, because the brakes were shot, I was a cartoon girl in a cartoon car. Halfway up, I was still pregnant, driving the ragged car that growled with hunger when I pressed the pedal.

I saw the tiger cat out of the corner of my eye and did not hit it. Instead, I drove into what felt like a wall. A woman screamed or a parrot shrieked. I pictured a diabetic woman, my mother perhaps, falling. A liquid wave of tenderness washed over my face, had something to do with the cat.

In the rearview mirror, how quickly gray, fluffy clouds were closing in and turning the sky the color of a bruised eye. Pepper clouds, I thought. Pepper was inside there, not rain…

Later, the doctor who was talking to me about the "split between here and there" had blond hair. He looked like my first boyfriend, the one who took my virginity, the one who I still talked to in my mind.

There was nothing toxic about the environment here, the one I was in, he said.

"Do you believe in beasts?" he asked.

"Yes," I said. "Hitler, of course. All beasts are people."

The doctor held up two twigs. One was me and the other looked like my twin. The other me was a stronger specimen, not yet bent or ruined.

SOUP AND TV

I stand near the boiling stockpot warming my fingers while the chicken and vegetables melt, the smell making our apartment strong. Canned wind howls from the TV screen in the living room, emitting a cool glow. He loves man-against-nature shows, which are actually a buff-looking male model talking to himself (and his hidden film crew) before lunch, which is probably catered sushi. I serve him the fresh broth on a lockable tray, move his legs from couch to floor, bend my knees to avoid using my back. He drinks soup with a special deep spoon—and though his fingers tremble, they are able to grasp. I sit with him, cheek against his warm shoulder, watching the man trapped between two icy mountain ranges build a fire out of sticks.

DELIVERY

Tony delivered all the pizza orders to the people out near the ocean path. No other place delivered this far from downtown. Tony did that for us, six nights a week, in his Honda Fit. His brother Richard had recently died in a car wreck, and before that, Tony and Richard tag-teamed. Tony's father owned the restaurant.

He'd hand me five extra takeout menus and say, "For your lucky lovers."

The women at the dog park would hassle each other about him. The dog park chicks called him "Hot-slice."

One evening, after a delivery, he asked me if he could smoke on my front steps, and I said, "You never need to ask, just light up and have one, and can I join you?" I was eating delivered pizza every night just to see him.

After he left, I brought out a roll of paper towels and cleaned my front steps of pollen, dust, and disgusting little insects. I wondered where my pride had been all these years, why I hadn't wanted my front door to seem friendly and charming.

Another night, I invited him in to share the Vegetarian without onions. He said he had nothing else to do, no more deliveries to make. We sat in the living room and didn't say a lot. What felt important was enjoying the pizza, his pizza, my pizza. Pizza that had been delivered to me by him and now eaten with him.

"I love the thicker crust," I said, taking a slice. He nodded his head. "It's so, so gooey," I added, and he smiled at my face.

He told me I was pretty and asked me if I liked green olives or black olives better.

I said, "I hate green, but love black," which was absolutely true. He kissed me, and I tasted black olives in his mouth. I imagined black olive wreaths on his brother's casket. I wanted to taste them strongly. I knew what sad men needed.

He left the next morning. During the night, when he was asleep and I should have been, I walked around and looked at his things. Leather jacket. His cell phone. It felt warm.

WHY NOT NOW?

A few years after my divorce, I joined a dating site full of bearded men. The dating site's criteria seemed to be that all of the men had beards. This was the opposite of my ex, who kept his hair military-short and distrusted fuzz of any kind around the mouth area.

A few men responded to me the very first week. I said on my profile page that I wanted a man who would enjoy eating lots of home-made soup. This was true, I loved soup-making. When it rained, I'd double the amount of soup I made. But lately, there was so much soup I had to throw it out, which made me sad.

I was most excited about a man named Joshua S. He had two children and was divorced; his beard was long, silky-looking and gentle. His eyes spoke of distant islands and dreams he had yet to dream.

I believed I may be able to squeeze into one of his dreams, and agreed to meet with him on Tuesday at one for coffee at the Who Knows Why? I liked the Who Knows Why? I liked the way none of the waitresses were pretty, and had decided that it was the ideal place to meet a man for a date.

I spent a few hours preparing my body. First, I bathed in sea salt. Then I slathered my face with butter from virginal coconuts. Not the kind from trees, the other kind. The kind you pay so much for, then you glow. I was glowing.

I applied musk oil, found the only pair of jeans in town that made my ass look like a strawberry, and felt ready to drive to the Who Knows Why? On my way out the door, the phone rang, and it was Joshua S.

Hello there, I am on my way, I said.

I am so sorry, I will have to cancel our date.

Oh, that's fine, fine, I said. I liked to be easygoing.

Yes, he said, my daughter needs a ride to the dentist. How about we do this some other time?

I was happy he suggested it.

After that, I lounged about on my hairy sofa smelling like soup and feeling silky, hoping the week would go by quickly. I liked the idea of a man who cared about his daughter's teeth enough to cancel a date. I was already set on him and wondered if we shouldn't meet at the other coffee shop, the one with the gorgeous waitresses. I thought it would make more sense, that kind of love test, and texted him to say, *Are we on for next week?*

He still hasn't texted back. In the meantime, I keep looking at my phone, imagining the way his words will pop out all over my screen, like unexpected fireworks.

PROBABLY, I'LL MARRY YOU

When Johan proposes, I'm out in the yard, watering plants. I'm not thinking about my situation, or about Johan, or about getting remarried.

That is when Johan shuffles from the house barefoot and shirtless, sinks to his knees.

I worry about him staining his khakis on the wet grass. Usually it's oil stains, tomato sauce, ink…

He can't care for a pair of pants. Can't hold a job. Thinking about his lack of employment gives me a headache, one that lingers over my right eye. I'm not employable either, that is, my eyes twitch in job interviews.

My ex-husband was a workhorse, never lost a job. Kept his pants real nice. Had a Grecian nose. The woman my husband left me for has a piggish, squashed-in nose. I have two arms, and my nose is terrific.

I can feel my stomach bubble up. Johan is looking at me with a smile that stretches around his smile lines. He has a cute, rat-like face. Rats are very intelligent animals. My best friend, Mancy, has two. When I visit her, one of them, a female, snuggles inside my shirt pocket. Rat pee dries quickly and there is almost no smell.

"You and I should get married," Johan says.

His face looks bloodless. The flowers in my yard are wilting, the lavatera is dying.

"No, wait," I say. "God, this is sudden."

I grab his hand.

"Lice," he says. "Otherwise I would kiss you."

Johan has lice from a hat he bought at the Salvation Army.

"Probably," I say.

"Probably….what?"

"Probably, I'll marry you."

If I were to start smoking again, this would be the moment.

"Well, think about it," Johan says.

He sticks his index finger on the bulls-eye center of his forehead, as though pointing at it with a loaded gun. It makes a mark on his skin. I can tell he is hoping not to jinx us.

EGG FOOT

My friend's wife is stuck at home because her feet stopped working. Otherwise she'd be going places. She calls her condition "Egg Foot." "Incurable," she says. "Unless treated." This she tells me in an email after her husband has flown. I google "Egg Foot" and after stumbling upon countless foot fetish photos, I stop. But maybe because of the strange photos, I can't help imagining her foot on my stomach, toes digging in, warm and crazy.

"She's insane," my friend says about his wife. "You just figuring this out?" I don't have many friends, and the ones I have are crackers. But I like my friend's batty wife. Privately, in my mind, I call her "Daisy."

"What will you do with your wolf pack in the city?" I ask my friend.

"Why don't you come along?" he replies, knowing I won't.

I don't say anything. Over the years, he's become angrier and fatter. I've become skinnier and dumber.

Daisy has shiny masses of white hair. He says she sleeps all day. He says this is great, in its own way, how they live completely different lives in the same house. I imagine taking her into my arms, smoothing down her petals. "How about that marriage of yours?" I'd say. "Incurable," she'd whisper.

We are all incurable, Daisy, I say to myself, trying to think of anything else.

FROM *THE DOG SEATED NEXT TO ME*
(2019)

TO-DO LIST

1. Wake adolescent with softest mom voice, tell her it's time to get up and ready for school. She hates to be late, even ten seconds, because she hates to be noticed.

2. Cereal and orange juice are ready, you say.

3. Cut puzzle pieces of parboiled meat for sick cat, microwave low, reanimate, sprinkle cat vitamins, serve on cat tree.

4. Measure out dog food, mix with pumpkin and green beans for dog diet.

5. Use kitty voice. Isolate other cat in bathroom with stars of kibble.

6. Prepare for drive to school by finding keys and sunglasses in purse despite the stain remover stick, planet stickers, half-eaten food bar, lavender hand sanitizer. Hiding like thieves, keys often play this game forever.

7. Talk to dog about losing things all the time. He is the most well-adjusted creature in the house. Offer volume discount for this service itemized as "dog love" (note to self—always talk to dog).

8. Calm the surly adolescent who used to be your adoring child.

9. Put on function face, lip color, deflate hair with water—forgive it.

SIREN

There is a flustered buffalo in a hotel bed, and it is a man, and it is a man who wants me so much he is levitating like an endangered animal. He is mastering the art of being made extinct. I am that kind of pony, here today, gone tomorrow, all fancy and prancing and cruel. I administer pleasure and then disappear, because I can, because I am a splinter, that is all I am when not making an animal happy.

There are the ones to take inside and to rock like babies, to rock until they groan and ask for pancakes.

There are ways to fly up against the heat of a man's sex, to singe his wings because nothing lasts longer than a good beer, or a fingerling potato on a cold night.

SURROUNDED BY WATER

"We live in a state surrounded by water," I'm saying to nobody in particular, mixing an amaretto sour.

"And most people never go to the beach," he finishes, as if he were my oldest friend.

Working in this bar for a while, making pretty good money, I'm still thinking one day I'll see him and know his face when he sits down.

"Did you want extra sour?" I ask.

"Perfect," he says, flipping his thick black bangs. "And when you catch a little break, you want to join me?"

"I don't sit with customers," I say. I always say.

Lou Anderson, deep into the regular, shouts, "She's too fucking important, she's a dancer."

"Nope," I say to black hair amaretto. "I'm just a nurse."

He smiles with tight-closed lips, salutes. We look at each other for a sec.

His phone rings, James Bond movie jingle. I giggle, then stop—his face whitening like a bleach stain.

"Hello…hello, wrong guy? Oh fuck off."

He looks into the deep, deep, deep of his phone.

"Pardon me," he tells an invisible human sitting next to him, throws the phone into the trash can—the trash can, rimming it, near the register.

"So, you're a real live dancer?" he asks me like I'm a black phone too.

I look through my eyelids to check who's around. If maybe Tim, the bouncer, sees. Tim's moving toward us in slow-mo, there's enough in my peripheral to breathe now, though I pee in my pants anyway. The other guys, my regulars, sit very still, sucking their skinny straws like air.

SPIDER

There's a spider in the bathroom, I tell him. It's six feet tall, I say. I wake him up and tell him to save me. I pee a few times a night and can't imagine slipping into the cold bathroom alone, facing this spider head-on. It's frigid here in Siberia. Outside, nothing can live for long. We humans and insects are all in the same boat, hoping for food, praying for love. Some people wander out and let the cold take care of their problems, let the cold win. Please, take care of Mr. Creepy, I say. My husband goes into the bathroom in his bare feet, hands in the air. He stands there, letting the spider crawl right up his leg, right up to his face. His skin is warm, the spider is happy. His legs are so long, perfect runways. They used to make me feel safe. "This cute little dot?" my husband says. He says this to me about our spider problem. He calls it a dot. "How would you feel if you were trapped in someone else's life?" he says.

SAAB STORY

"What are the chances of getting hit by a meteorite?" We were at Point Reyes seashore, had driven hours north of the city to watch the sunset. We drove to beautiful places in our untrustworthy car, wondering where and when it would die. "We live in the world's most perfect place," he'd remind me. "Except for earthquakes."

I wanted him to have a theory. To explain things to me. To me, our lives were worrisome, driving away from an apartment filled with unpaid bills to see another perfect sunset.

"I don't know anything about the statistical risk of death by meteorite," my husband said.

The Saab sounded asthmatic—creaky, loud. I thought about the man who sold it to us. Bruce. He told us he used to sell time shares before he sold cars.

"This car suits the two of you," he said.

His lips seemed to collapse on each other as he moved his mouth around. He was out of breath, fanning his face with a marketing flier. There was pressure on him to sell us a car, pressure on us to buy the cheapest car we could still feel safe in.

We parked by the sea. The sunset was so orange and exotic, a blanket of fluffy sky. We perched in our heated lemon, staring at the glow.

CURED

He tasted like a bologna sandwich. And it was not his breath. It felt like a taste that lived deep inside his body. She imagined he was still grieving. His young wife had died. This kind of sadness could turn a man's mouth into some kind of pickled meat.

They were meeting again, for the fourth time, at the coffee place. She with velvet socks, which made her feel lovable. This was something he couldn't know, wouldn't care to. How she wore velvet foot coverings. Little things like this. His brain couldn't yet digest much of her wonderfulness.

The cured-meat flavor theory made sense in the natural world. Tears were made of water and salt. Grief was not angular, it was soft, droopy, wet. One could soak in a pond full of it.

Humans, like amphibious animals, developed ugly traits to protect themselves. Some freaky African toad squirted blood from its eyes to offer, like a food sample, to predatory birds. This toad's blood tasted so bad, the birds flew the fuck home.

He was a harlequin toad to her, that kind of rare, beautiful creature, highly endangered. As time crept by, she wanted to marry him, take care of him, and hold him in the crook of her arm (where her cat slept, now) after diving in and out of the deep swamp of sex.

When they kissed, she felt well-preserved and lovely. Maybe this was the cured meat talking. Salted, which meant it would never expire. She thought about asking if he'd let her pour salad dressing on his tongue, but she'd never really ask this, he was dealing with enough.

She had always taken pride in being a messy lover, uninhibited. But here she was in love with a man who could not laugh, and she was going out of her mind. She felt like a spider, or a monkey, or a toad. She just so wanted to soap him up, get down to things.

Tired and hungry, she pulled on a mask of gentility and moderation. For the first time, after the first few martinis, she made an aggressive suggestion. "Hey, I'd like to head over to the Blue Towel. Wanna come?"

"Blue Towel, you say?"

"Yep, that's the place."

He followed her with no resistance. Seemed ready for something.

They staggered to her car. She took a group of dogs to the beach every day, so she had a blue dog towel in the backseat. It was an embarrassing towel. She washed it but not often.

"It smells like dogs in here," he said.

"Yes, it does."

He sneezed and sneezed. She pulled off one of her velvet socks and handed it to him, asked him to pet it, to feel it, smell it. He didn't register surprise. His face looked stretchy and sad. He had been sterilized by grief, and this needed to be undone.

TEA PARTY

Underground, a tea party has commenced—a city-full of Dumbo-eared family members.

"Your name was Tim," she reminded him. "Timothy. You and me were married."

She realized he had stopped listening and imagined him plunging down a hole or into a box.

"Okay, hold on…" She closed the box gently. Wrapped him in tissue paper recycled from Christmases past.

When your husband becomes a rodent, she typed into Google, hoping for simple instructions.

Long ago, he explained, his family carried disease. He was simply scurrying up the pipes, trying to get back home.

MOOD RING

When the sun came out, I took off five layers. I felt naked and free, ready to show him my ruined foot. It had changed again, like a mood ring, an ice-cold reminder right there in the middle of the living room. He'd just returned from his jog, twenty miles, and there was my foot. The room got still. My husband, the violinist, skinny and quick, a ferret. The room hot and sad, the sofa we'd picked because it was so cozy we just fit.

I kissed the top of his head. "Ouch!" he said. He used to have stacks of hair. I'm sorry, I said, but he knew this already. He was sorry too. Of course. He scooted away and looked out the window. His bald head was a magnet for beauty. There was a new woman on the block, with a Stradivarius body, the kind he had always wanted to play.

SETTLING

He took my hand, led me to the bathroom, opened the door and slipped in. The bathroom was dark. Through the partially opened window, an apartment with a yellow breakfast nook. His breath was on my mouth with the smell of fruit and white wine, sweet and sour sauce. This was where he felt safest; bathrooms, closets, tiny, ridiculous places.

Earlier that night, at a movie, I'd listened to him eating unbuttered popcorn. How each piece squeaked in his teeth. I believed I'd grow to hate this sound, and the idea made me want to plant my hand on his knee, which I did.

There were many ways to love, and to be loved, and none of them were just the way you dreamed as a child. My mother had been relieved to lounge around in an old, stained bathrobe, watch the news and fall asleep after my father left. Some people don't want the worries of entanglement, Mom had said. Some people prefer the music of their own lives.

BLUE-TONGUED SKINK

He wanted me to have a purpose in this world. Having a baby would get me out of bed and cooking, he said. Bending over, planning dinners. He probably also wanted me to be more awake, not just lying in bed, as I did most days.

Too late. I had put my money down on an exotic lizard. A baby did not sound nearly as interesting. The pet store had my deposit, and I was lying in bed planning my future with the blue-tongued skink. He lived at the store. They tended to be slow to adopt out. I just needed the glass cage and the UV lights, a large bag of sand, and an endless supply of insects. I had photos of skinks everywhere now, the inside and the outside of my phone. I was considering a reptile tattoo. All I could think about was how such cool, smooth skin would feel around my shoulder, like an arm, or a hand. How much warmer than anything else I might happen to love.

INFIDELITY

He watched her again that day, her face, her features, something that might change. The way she watched him back, eyes like blue dragonflies hovering near a rock. He brushed the hair from his eyes, tilted his face to the right like a chain-smoking waitress. What'll you have? he wanted to say. Chips with cheddar? Sex with a kiss? Words he could use with other women, but not with her.

He had nobody to talk to, and the words gathered in his throat like angry tourists, pushing each other out.

"Near the trail, I saw a yellow bird," he said. That sounded ignorant. Birds weren't yellow—they had a yellow breast or a yellow wing tip. There was no way to know if she heard, so he watched her mouth. Sometimes it looked cruel, other times it made him want to laugh. He stared at her nose, a long, crazy nose—so large it should have pulled her gaze down, but it balanced just right.

WHAT THE DOG THINKS

Today my human seemed to be chasing her tail. I mean, chasing herself into a bad mood. At eleven a.m. she was wearing her astral nightgown and her Jupiter slippers. She needed a project. I heard her say this to a few people on the phone. Did I mention her hair was really orange this time? It was only pretty at night.

When she talks on the phone, and I listen, it's not eavesdropping because she speaks so loudly. It can be heard all over the planet, a lot of what she says. And she was petting my head a bit during some of that conversation. She said, I'm tired of being a wife. It's not a job I'm good at.

She cried a bit, and the poor friend on the other end of the line must have been upset. She said she was nothing but a broken link, that she loved getting drunk in bars and being courted, that she had an uncontrollable fear of old people. That she was a horrible person, a horrible wife, a terrible daughter, ready to make a landing on a new betrayal every week. That is what she said.

It sounded true to me, but nobody knows what is true here. After she hung up, she hurried off to meet a man at the coffee shop. How do I know? I saw her put on green eye shadow, the color she swore hurried love along. She's nothing but rude when she primps, scooting me away. She's forgotten to love me so regularly now that I've started taking it from the fat white cat. This cat! She even loves my awful breath, says my bigness obscures the actual sensation. She follows me around these days, and I admit to liking it. But man, is she white—and fat!

THE WEEK I BECAME OLD

I met him for lunch at the Hive. He had black curly hair and a strained smile. I tried to relax, smoothed my skirt, patted my blouse down, moved my feet toward his.

I had become old just that week, no longer wanted to even try to be open, felt useless and befuddled. Yet I had found a space on the street away from the parking meters, two hours to get myself enlivened. It was a relief to see he was as anxious as me, with a scrunched look on his rootlike face. Was I taboo?

"Did you take the bus to get here?" he asked.

"No, I don't take the bus," I said. "Did you?" I didn't even know how to take a bus.

"No, I just came from work. I only have an hour. And then back to work. Sorry."

"No, that's okay," I said.

He started telling me his story. He was in the middle of a divorce, his wife had thrown him out—"like an overcooked noodle," he said, the way she threw out his old CDs, mementos, family photographs. "She finally—quote—uncluttered her life," he said. "I was one of the things she no longer wanted."

The energy flow between us was taking its time, trying not to aggravate our conditions, but it was happening. At that moment, I saw him in an old photograph. He reminded me of the sherbety days of high school, the salty skin of the first boy I had kissed behind the library. And the second boy, and the third boy, and the fourth boy I had kissed behind the library, as though I were becoming a technician, a kissing scientist. Until somebody alerted my mother about my "problem." After which the kisses stayed with me, slid into my pockets like gum wrappers.

And yet this man was ruined. Thrown out, discarded. His wife had been holding him, and she was ready to move on.

SHOW BUSINESS

Yesterday I almost tripped over a man lying in the road. "What is wrong with you?" I asked.

"Show business," he said. He was not exaggerating—his eyes were really just holes with marbles in them.

He told me about his ex-girlfriend, a woman he'd met on the stage, an actress and dancer. "Her eyes were homes of silent prayer to me," he said. Water dripped down from his holes.

I felt I could tell him anything, and so I did. My boyfriend had an awful way of making a living, I said. He juggled stunned live birds and then got rid of them. "Juggling living birds for crowds," I said.

He shook little white petals from his shirt and stood up. "I won't be had," he said.

"Neither will I," I said. And then we held hands, and made promises we'd someday break.

WHAT THE DOCTOR ORDERED

The last appointment, my doctor popped the question—asked me to pet-sit and house-sit for him while he traveled to Florence, described his wooded wonderland cottage on Mount Tamalpais and his arthritic dog, Jeeves.

I'm dying very quickly, and the sweet chemicals in candy and diet sodas are comforting, so the first thing I think about is if there would be a convenience store nearby, so deep in the woods. Nobody believes I'm dying from such a sad and rare disorder, one that doesn't have a name. Only the doctor knows what is really wrong with me, but he says there is no name for this fatal illness.

Sometimes, he'll begin, "You see…" then change the trail of the conversation to something as impersonal as the local deer population crisis.

"Well, yes of course they are a menace to gardens," I say, "but they don't look evil, that's what is so damn sad, I bet." He doesn't answer, which makes me worry that he would shoot them. I tell myself he wouldn't, being a natural healer.

He said this is a lonely pilgrimage—off to Florence to say goodbye to his former fiancée, a well-known visual artist named Sandra who has a rare and fatal blood disease. Her illness has a name, but the name is very long and Latin, and he can't pronounce it. He said it would be easier to sing it, says, "Bella, bella" when he speaks of her.

"I can take care of the doggie and cottage," I said, wanting him to perk. He stroked his beard sweetly, as if it were a bunny. I wanted to touch all of the doctor's things. I wanted to lie in his sheets.

I've done many things the doctor will not approve of since moving in, like turning on the heat in the frigid mornings and removing his aggressive wind chimes. I am bored with his beautiful house, the whimsical trickle of a natural creek in the yard that honest-to-God polliwogs swim in. I'm on Pluto, or maybe I have landed in Carmel before it was ruined and turned into a theme park. I hate authentic character, I've decided, the master bedroom smelling like vintage sweat and pine, salty stuff I'll never smell fresh from his skin unless I grab him while he's jogging, in which case I would risk being abandoned as his patient.

I feel annoyed by his creviced leather sofa, forest-green corduroy chairs, Pennsylvania Dutch braid rugs. The only bright spot is Jeeves, the doctor's ten-year-old Golden Retriever who follows me everywhere wishing I were the doctor. We have talks about why the doctor dresses so well, when all the other doctors look schlumpy. "Do you think he's vain?" I ask Jeeves, who looks unsure about everything.

I'm not getting enough fruit, he'd say, am getting sick from energy bars and Diet Cokes. I am often thinking about what it would be like to be naked under the llama rug when the doctor gets home all stricken with grief.

Since living in the doctor's cottage, I've been imagining the shape of his fingers while chopping vegetables. Picking just one finger would be hard, like selecting a puppy from a box. Some people fall into the trap of the rice farmer obsessed with growing apples. And it's true, I've grown and cultivated men all my life, but this one will not thrive in my soil. It's time to move on.

I water each of the doctor's daisy bushes carefully, do not flood their roots. I talk to his plants so they don't die while he's gone. Jeeves waddles out and plunks next to me to sit in the sun.

WHAT THE DEAD WANT

There are so many dead people in her life, especially in this house. They float around and exaggerate. They want to see something sexy. That nightgown? they say. They miss eating berries. They're sure she'll be okay. They say wonderful things about what you might do here on earth. They should have taken more lovers, had more beach weekends, seen more foreign films. They ask for autographs from the living.

INTEGRITY

Nance lost her integrity years ago when she slept with everyone but promised them nothing. It would have been more sensible to promise them something but never sleep with them.

Her smile was the thing. It reminded people of their grandmothers or their favorite nieces. Familiar but provocative. She'd loved being alive. She had felt that this was what she'd been put on earth to do, to confuse other humans.

By the time she was diagnosed, she had lost her husband. To him, it made no sense. The weirdness of it all. Nonsense, like a husband and wife who get a divorce even though they love each other.

* * *

And then, after years on her own, Nance met Bob. Bob had been recruited to help plant a tree in a neighbor's yard.

Nance's ex had not been handy, couldn't even put up a shelf without breaking it. Did that mean she shouldn't miss him?

She waved at the tree-planting man on the way to her car, determined to stop confusing men with sex. She woke up all sparkly-eyed and ready to hit the ground, determined not to confuse anyone. It was about as exciting as getting up before dawn to tackle the tax forms.

* * *

Bob was, no doubt, married. In the old days that meant Nance would plot to seduce him.

She'd confuse a man on his wedding day. Or in the middle of an anniversary. Her smile would make a man lose his bearings or feel he already knew her, sure he'd slept with her already so it wouldn't count.

Bob had such a warm look, Nance was ready to say hello—nicely, sisterly—while checking his ring finger. You might have said she was ready to begin again.

SOUR FRUIT

Her neighbor came over with a bag of lemons, camped in the hall and watched her make tea in the kitchen. She was wearing slippers and her husband was out for an eighteen-hour run, training for an eighty-mile race. It was always about lemons for anyone who lived on the block. The trees here were so full of sour fruit it intimidated people; he said the lemons were fierce. And really, it wasn't a good idea, wouldn't fly, to keep bringing her lemons when she was alone. She didn't know what to do with them and she thought it might be more interesting to do more.

I like it when a woman knows what to do. This is what she imagined him saying. She wished he had said this, that this was just exactly what he had said.

And she wished she were the kind of woman who could squeeze a lemon for him with her lips, and have him watch, and then to hear him ask for sugar and a spoon.

She did not think of herself as a fanatic; she had a bit of OCD, really, just the normal kind of lust, she knew he wanted this. She wanted him to drink fruit juice, not whiskey, and to hold her hand, and to tell her he would be okay. And to kiss her while he told her she would be okay. And then he would say, *Will I also be okay?* And she would say of course. Even if she lied.

This was the kind of human she needed in her kitchen.

SOMETHING SHE NEEDED
TO KNOW

The boy in third grade who left a Mickey Mouse ring and a love note in her desk. The garage door with thousands of spiders' nests, nobody to wash them down. Her mother looking different in California, hair tipped blonde, smoking near the telephone. Her father in Maryland, the wrinkled map of his hands. Sneaking out of the house at dawn, hoping to get kidnapped, to be returned to sender. The boy pulling her into the bathroom, telling her she could watch. Butter stains on clothing, the gift for ruining things, even the potted cactus. The plane to Pennsylvania, landing in snow, the hearse carrying her father to a perfect hole. Her cousin so changed with new huge breasts, glaring at her mother. Her aunt saying Why did you treat him like that? God's voice in the dark of the hotel room, talking to her while her mother snored away. Songs on the radio like "Take Me in Your Arms and Rock Me," something she needed to know. Her father's moon face smiling from so many brown frames on the wall: holding a dog, holding a trophy, being a boy before growing up into her terrible parent. How she would have wanted to play with him then. And the warm way she feels when she thinks of the peeing boy's body. How her father, in the form of different boys, would always make her watch.

MOVING ON

She notices him walking a madcap new dog, the one he adopted after the old one died. She puffs her cheeks into a smile. In the city, strangers don't speak. They imitate porcupines. The quills come out. They bubble, shape their mouths into lines.

This new dog doesn't look likely to ever become gentle like the old dog. She approves. She believes you have to dispose of the past, that dogs are like ex-husbands. Moving on is critical. And yet this new dog really seems wrong, bucking against the man's leash, bouncing as if possessed.

This can happen to anyone. There are problems with remembering dogs we once loved, dogs we will never walk again.

* * *

Her new husband snores demurely on his side of the bed, wrapped up in a burrito of sheets. She can't find his skin. She lies there awake, thinking about the ex. No matter how bad their problems were, she could always relax in the smell and the warmth of his skin: he never tamaled himself away. He'd hold her tight against his shoulder until morning. At some point this became intolerable—that only his nocturnal shoulder made them happy together, that by day they'd fight. She told him it made no sense to confuse matters that way. He agreed and withdrew, moving into the living room for the next two years, sleeping alone with his shoulder empty while they went through the divorce.

* * *

Over at Clownfish, the new downtown sushi joint, she's sitting alone, staring at the fish tornado, proud of herself for taking control.

Sometimes she sits around the house feeling sorry for herself until she gets a craving for crab. Nothing wrong with being hungry. Hunger presents the opportunity for fullness. She's thankful for the existence of crab legs, the hidden, perfect meat inside.

INFESTATION

There was a large cockroach living in my heart, clinking its tender little legs, plotting escape. People's hearts are heavy with bugs they won't admit. Mine remembered everything—the early days of my marriage, dreams of growing old while holding fingers. Driving to Monterey, after his affair, I told my husband about the cockroach. "Smart, but not very optimistic," I said.

There's something about driving to a beautiful place, not looking directly at each other, watching the highway. He said, "I understand. There's a cockroach inside me too."

That night, I felt the tiniest part of me scurrying out, eager to be seen. His sudden disclosure had made my head spin. Under the motel sign, I heard two hearts chirping. We made love for the first time in years, the angels trying to bring us back to each other, as if they recognized a friend in the dark.

LOST TOURIST

It was her high school boyfriend who started the trouble. She was just sixteen. He suggested she didn't have a normally shaped vagina, his finger skittering around it like a lost tourist.

"You need to see a doctor. Find out why it isn't opening," he said.

"God, that's embarrassing."

He shrugged and turned on the TV. Animal Planet.

"That's what doctors are for," he said. "I can't do much in there. Not if it's all sewn up."

You could say this was how things started with her mother's landscaper. She was waiting in line to order a double mint chip cone at McConnel's, wondering what to do about her problem, and there he was, in line right in front of her.

He saw her too. Smiled. These days, men sprouted out of unlikely places, like weeds from invisible cracks in walls.

He pointed to his apartment complex. "I live right over there," he said.

"You live near some very dangerous ice cream," she said, and he laughed. That night, she jogged over to his apartment.

"Thank you for such a pleasant distraction," he said, letting her inside.

On Saturday, the boyfriend scratched himself like a flea-ridden dog on her beanbag chair.

"I wonder if we will ever try that again. I'm beginning to worry," he said.

"Don't worry," she said.

She felt tired and happy. Sloppy and carefree. When she went to kiss him, his lips felt slippery, like a snail's road home.

UNCLE SHUG'S

At Uncle Shug's, we're in love with each other again. Laughing, loving each other's faces. We're the funny kids nobody ever wants to be away from, like siblings, but with sex. He's me and I'm him. I sit on his lap, and he doesn't look around to see if his mother is watching, making him feel too guilty to breathe. Here in Uncle Shug's we're sharing key lime pie, and I'm feeling his warm fine skin, and I'm kissing the places where his golden hair used to be. He's calling me Vixen of the Outer Sunset, kissing my lips the way he did before his mother's car accident, before he curled up inside himself after I was mugged.

We order Cokes. Remember these sugary cravings? I say, pretty sure I'm dreaming this whole thing up. We're divorced now, right?

That's okay, he says. I'm digging this dream, how we're in it together, the way we were in the beginning. Don't smother it with too much thinking, vixen.

Under the table, our feet find each other. I wiggle my toes beneath his fine, fungal nails. What's next? I say. I'm covered with glaze, just like the honey-baked ham he used to slice up on Christmas morning. Here we are, boneless. Here we are, young and funny and in love with the world. Here we are, waiting till the hand-cut potatoes arrive.

ABOUT THE AUTHOR

Meg Pokrass is the author of nine collections of flash fiction and two novellas in flash. Her work has been published in three Norton anthologies, including Flash Fiction America, New Micro, and Flash Fiction International; The Best Small Fictions 2018, 2019, 2022, and 2023; Wigleaf Top 50; and hundreds of literary magazines, including *Electric Literature, New England Review, McSweeney's, Five Points, Split Lip, Washington Square Review*, and *Passages North*. Meg is the founding editor of *New Flash Fiction Review*, festival curator of Flash Fiction Festival UK, and founding/managing editor of the *Best Microfiction* anthology series. She lives in Scotland, where she serves as chief judge for the Edinburgh Flash Fiction Award.